A King Production presents…

A Novel

Joy Deja King

ISBN 13: 978-1942217220
ISBN 10: 1-942217-22-6
Cover concept by Joy Deja King & www.MarionDesigns.com
Cover layout and graphic design by www.MarionDesigns.com
Cover Model: Joy Deja King
Typesetting: Linda Williams
Editor: Dolly Lopez & Linda Williams

Library of Congress Cataloging-in-Publication Data;
King, Deja
Trife Life To Lavish: a novel/by Joy Deja King
For complete Library of Congress Copyright info visit
www.joydejaking.com

A King Production
P.O. Box 912, Collierville, TN 38027

A King Production and the above portrayal log are trademarks of A King Production LLC

This Book is Dedicated To My:

Family, Readers and Supporters.

I LOVE you guys so much. Please believe that!!

A KING PRODUCTION

Trife Life To Lavish

JOY DEJA KING

Prologue
Escaping the Madness
Charlotte, North Carolina The Past...

"Get the fuck outta my house!" Teresa screamed, as she stood in the entrance of the bedroom door. Teresa's initial reaction was to drag the woman lying on her back out of the bed, but seeing the horrific shock on the woman's face made her quickly reassess that decision. Teresa and the other woman both seemed to be stuck on pause, and the only person being on fast forward was the man who continued getting his stroke on as if nothing was going to stop him from busting a nutt.

"Oh shit! I'm almost there!" the man moaned, speeding up his pace as if oblivious to the fact that he had a viewing audience.

Teresa couldn't believe she was watching as her husband fucked another woman right in front of her face. Immediately, flashback images consumed her. She thought back to all the bullshit she had been enduring for the last six years.

In the beginning, Kevon seemed to be Teresa's saving grace. She had a baby girl, who was just over a year old, had no money, no job and a bleak future. The landlord had given her an eviction notice, and Teresa was going to have to go live with her mother so she and her baby wouldn't be homeless. But that never happened, because Kevon swooped in and took on the role as her man, and a father to her daughter, Genevieve. Teresa was so enamored, that when Kevon asked that she and the baby come back to live with him at his crib in Charlotte, she packed up and left Philly, the only place she had ever called home.

Teresa felt like she had died and gone to suburban heaven, when she first arrived at the handsome two-story brick house on the tree-lined street. She had grown accustomed to living in drug infested project buildings with hallways smelling like piss, and where trash replaced grass as landscaping. Inhaling the fresh, clean air in the south seemed like a life she would only daydream about, not actually live.

But Teresa's daydreaming quickly turned into a never-ending nightmare after marrying Kevon. He was no longer her saving grace, but instead the cause of her demise.

"What the fuck is you doing here? I thought you wasn't gonna be home for another hour," Kevon spit, after finally busting a nutt and pulling himself out of the stiffened woman.

Teresa's mind was so far gone with reflecting

on the horrors of the past, that at first she didn't hear her husband.

"Bitch, don't you hear me talking to you?" Kevon continued.

"Nigga, fuck you!" Teresa barked, coming out her daze. "You so damn trifling, you gon' bring another woman in my house and fuck her in my bed? I'm so sick of your disrespectful bullshit, I don't know what to do!"

"I swear I had no idea he was married, or that this was your home!" the fear stricken girl who looked no more than eighteen said, pleading her case to Teresa. She jumped out of bed, scrambling to get her clothes on, in an attempt to escape without the ass whooping she assumed his wife was about to put on her.

But unbeknownst to the teeny bopper, Teresa was beginning to grow so immune to her husband's revolting behavior, that she refused to waste her energy on beating any of his women down. Plus, she believed the girl when she said she was clueless to Kevon's marital status. This here situation needed to be handled with one person—her husband.

"You ain't got to explain shit to her! This *my* house. It ain't my fault she brought her ass back home early."

Teresa stood with her eyes twitching. *This nigga is determined to have a throw-down up in this mutherfucka, and I'ma give it to him!* "Little girl, I think it's best you go. I need to deal with my husband."

The girl nodded her head in agreement with Teresa's request, and leaped up to make an exit.

"I'll call you later on," Kevon said, casually, making it clear he wasn't pressed about how pissed Teresa was.

"Ma, who was that woman that just ran up out of here?"

Teresa looked down at her seven-year-old daughter. With all the anger consuming her, she had forgotten she was there. "Genevieve, baby, she was nobody. You go to your bedroom and close the door. I got some things to handle with your father."

Genevieve looked over at her father as he stood in only his boxer shorts, before asking, "Daddy, is everything okay?"

"I'm good," he answered, pulling out a box of cigarettes from his pants pocket and grabbing a pack of matches off the dresser to light up.

"Genevieve, g'on to your room and color or something. I'll be there in a minute."

"But I'm hungry."

Teresa slit her eyes at her daughter, not in the mood for no whining. "I'ma tell you one more time to go to your room," Teresa said, in a threatening tone that Genevieve knew all too well. "I'ma make you something to eat when I'm done in here. Now g'on!"

Genevieve looked back at her daddy, then her mom, before walking out their room. But instead of going to her bedroom like she was told, she sat down in the hallway corner, determined to find out what had her mother so angry.

"Teresa, I don't feel like hearing whateva bullshit 'bout to come out yo' mouth," Kevon said, slipping on his jeans.

"You should'a thought about that before you brought some young ass girl up in this house!"

"Oh, would it make you feel better if I would'a brought some old ass woman up in here to fuck? I mean, I'm just saying…"

"You know what, Kevon? Why don't you pack up your shit and get the fuck out. Clearly this ain't where you wanna be no more, so I think it's best you leave."

Kevon gave a low chuckle before taking a pull off the cigarette and laying it down in the ashtray. "I hope you ain't been dabbling in my stash, because only some powerful yang can have you speaking out the side of your neck like that. 'Cause I ain't going no motherfuckin' where."

"Well, you won't be staying up in here with me with this disrespectful bullshit. I'm tired, Kevon. From you getting other bitches pregnant, having ho's stashed up in apartments, to them blowing up my phone looking for you. Now, you so sloppy wit' yo' shit, you bringing broads to the place I lay my head. I can't live like this! I won't live like this!"

"Bitch, have you forgotten where I found your busted ass at? You was a broke-down ho, with not even one dollar to your name. You didn't even have enough money to buy milk or pampers for your baby. If it wasn't for me, you and Genevieve would still be in Philly, struggling just to get by. So save all that 'you can't live like this'. You better be happy you gotta place to live."

"Oh really? You don't want to leave? Then I'll leave, 'cause anything is better than this." Teresa turned to walk away, facing the fact that she was fighting a useless cause.

"Where the fuck you think you going?" Kevon yanked Teresa's arm, stopping her from walking away.

"Get the fuck off of me! I told you I'm done wit' this shit."

"Nah, we ain't done until I say we done. I been taking care of you and a child that ain't even mine, and you think you gon' just leave me? You fuckin' crazy! That's not how this shit work. I pulled you out of those projects and made an honest woman outta you, so you owe me your life just for that."

"I don't owe you shit! And if I did, I've paid my debt in full having to deal wit' all your drama over the years. Now, get the fuck off of me! I'm taking my daughter and getting the fuck outta here."

The next thing Teresa knew, she was hitting the floor from the impact of the punch Kevon landed on her face. *This nigga been cheating on me for all these years, now he wanna put his hands on me too! Aahh, hell no!* Teresa thought as she lay on the floor staring up at the man she once believed was the best thing that ever happened to her.

"You see what you made me do? I've been nothing but a provider for you and Genevieve, and this is the respect I get. That's why you gotta treat women like hos and tricks, 'cause ya' don't 'preciate nothing. But you my wife, and you will respect me."

"Kevon, get away from me! I promised myself

I would neva let another man put their hands on me, and I meant that shit!"

Kevon grabbed Teresa by her hair and dragged her over near the dresser. Teresa was swinging her arms and kicking her legs, irate and scared, not knowing what Kevon was going to do next. But Kevon was undeterred.

"You think you gon' talk shit to me in my house where I pay the bills? I don't give a fuck if you caught me up in this crib everyday wit' a different bitch, you show me respect. But just like you gotta beat obedience in your children, I'ma put the fear of God in you," he said, grabbing the still lit cigarette from the ashtray.

"Kevon, no-o-o-o-o-o!" Teresa screamed out as little pieces of ashes were falling down, barely missing her exposed skin.

"Ain't no use in screaming now. You should'a thought about that shit before running off at the mouth." Kevon lifted Teresa up off the floor like a rag doll. Her petite frame dangled in the air as Kevon pointed the cigarette towards her face. "Now, where shall I leave my mark? Some place where you can constantly look at, as a reminder that you'll always be my bitch."

All anyone could hear were the gut wrenching cries of pain as Kevon mashed the cigarette into the upper right side of Teresa's left breast.

Before he released her hair and Teresa dropped to the floor, she caught a glimpse of the devilish smirk on Kevon's face. The pain was overwhelmingly excruciating, but seeing the gratified look on her husband's mug as he was leaving her there to suffer gave Teresa the strength to fight back. With his back turned, believing she was in no condition to defend herself, Teresa grabbed the marble lamp off the nightstand, and with all her might, slammed it over Kevon's head, not once, not twice, but three times.

Exhausted from using all her strength, Teresa let the lamp drop out of her hands, and when she looked up, she saw her daughter, Genevieve standing only feet away with a blank stare on her face. Teresa then looked down at Kevon, and blood was pouring from the open gash on his head.

"Oh shit, he's dead!" Teresa mumbled, as she shook his rigid body, looking for any sign of life.

"Ma, is Daddy dead? Did you kill Daddy?"

"This man here, ain't none of your Daddy," Teresa said, firmly latching onto her daughter's arm.

Genevieve's eyes filled with tears. She heard the harsh words exchanged between her parents, but didn't want to believe they were true. Kevon was the only father she'd known, and although he didn't treat her mother well all the time, for the most part, he had been decent towards her. But now her mother was affirming the worst; Kevon wasn't her father, and now he was dead.

"I can't believe you killed my Daddy!" Genevieve said, under sniffles, still unable to call him anything else.

"Didn't you hear what I said? That man ain't none of your Daddy!" Teresa screamed, pointing to the dead body. "Now hush up with that crying! I need to think." Teresa's hands were shaking and her head throbbing.

She wanted to get away from Kevon and leave him with some of the pain he had caused her, but murder was never part of the equation.

"Ma, what you gon' do?"

"You mean what *we* gon' do? We getting the hell outta here. Go to your room and pack up as much stuff you can fit in here," Teresa ordered, opening the closet door and handing her daughter a suitcase.

"But I don't wanna leave Daddy like this!" The tears were now flowing down Genevieve's face.

"Look at me. I said, look at me!" Teresa yelled, holding her daughter tightly. She knelt down on the floor so she could be eye level with Genevieve. "I know you scared, baby, so am I. But mommy had to defend herself. I didn't mean to kill Kevon, it was an accident, but the police probably wouldn't believe me. I would go to jail and they would send you away to some foster home. I don't want to lose you, baby, so we have to leave."

"And go where, Ma?"

"I'm not sure, but somewhere far away, where nobody knows us or can find us. All we have is each other now, so please, baby, don't fight me. Do what Mommy says. Go to your room and pack up your things. I'll come get you when it's time to go."

Genevieve looked over at Kevon and back into the eyes of her mother. She grabbed the suitcase and left the room.

Teresa wanted to break down and cry, not to mourn the death of her husband, but because she knew her life would never be the same again. She spent the next hour packing up her belongings and trashing the place. When Kevon's body was discovered, she hoped that it would appear as if someone had broken in looking for either money or drugs. It was known in the streets of Charlotte that Kevon was heavily involved with the drug game, and other illegal activities.

Before Teresa left, she grabbed the murder weapon and wrapped it up in a towel before putting it in one of her bags. She then went to Kevon's closet and took the money he always kept in a pair of Timberland boots. She knew Kevon had another spot where he stashed his drugs and real paper, but had no idea exactly where it was, nor did she have the time to try and figure it out. The money Teresa took wasn't enough to ball, but it would hold them over until they found a new home.

"Genevieve, it's time to go, baby," Teresa said, calmly. She held her daughter's hand and looked around the place she'd called home for years. Not only would their lives change, but so would their names. Teresa and Genevieve no longer existed, she decided, closing the door and escaping the madness.

Queens, New York
The Present...
10 Years Later
Letting Go

To embrace what the future holds, you have to first be able to let go of what keeps you holding on to the past. But many could attest, that simple request is much easier said than done.

"Ma, Daddy's dead... You killed Daddy! No-o-o-o! Daddy can't be dead!" Nichelle yelled out, fighting the demons in her sleep.

"Nichelle, wake up! Wake up, Nichelle!" her mother said, trying to shake her daughter out of her nightmare.

Nichelle swung her arms wildly, causing her mother to grab her sweat-drenched body tightly to help her escape the dark place she'd succumbed to. "You killed my Daddy!" she continued to scream out, not able to free herself from the dream that would engulf her mind every few months.

"That's enough, Nichelle! Now wake up!" her mother barked, pushing her down on the bed as she covered her mouth.

"Why did you have to kill Daddy," Nichelle

mumbled as she finally found her way back from the horror she was clinging on to. Tears were fighting there way down her cheeks, and all her mother could do was hug her daughter, knowing the wounds of the past were still fresh and unhealed.

It had been ten years since Teresa took her daughter and left her deadly secret behind in North Carolina, but unfortunately, it wasn't as easy for Genevieve to bury. Teresa had done everything, from changing their names, to Nichelle and Sheila, to moving to another state, to trying to reprogram her daughter to forget about that dreadful day, but when it seemed that all had been forgotten, Genevieve would have one of her episodes and bring the skeletons of the past to the present. As soon as she thought she had long buried Teresa and Genevieve, Nichelle would resurrect them.

"Baby, you have to let go and stop having these nightmares. If somebody ever heard you, they would start asking questions, and I don't even want to think about what that might lead to."

"I'm sorry, Ma."

"You have to quit being sorry and just stop! It's been ten years, and you keep rehashing that shit like it happened yesterday."

"What do you expect? It ain't every day that a seven-year-old witnesses her mother killing her father."

"Oh Lord, here we go again! I can't do this no more, Nichelle. We have been through this so many damn times I feel like you have me on repeat. Now, please let it go. You've had more than enough time to get over it...I have."

"I hear you."

"I hope so, because all I need is for you to go ruining some shit."

"Ain't nobody ruining nothing. I've held this secret for all this time, and ain't nothing gon' change. I mean, besides Carmelo and Tierra, you all the family I have. I don't want to lose you too."

Sheila looked down and shook her head in frustration before standing up. "Get some sleep, baby. You have school in the morning," she said, turning off the light in Nichelle's bedroom.

After she closed the door, Sheila went to her own bedroom and sat down trying to unload the anger and guilt she had towards her daughter. She was angry that Nichelle wouldn't let go of the past, but at the same time she felt guilty that her daughter had to carry the burden of her sins for all these years. She had no idea if or when Nichelle would be able to let go.

"I need five hundred dollars, not tomorrow, not next week, but right now!" Tierra snapped, as she put on her Baby Phat denim jumper.

"What?"

"I didn't stutter. I need them coins. You been promising me the money for two weeks, and I'm still standing here with my hand out trying to make it rain. So you need to come off that money, like now." Tierra stood staring at Radric with her arms crossed and lips poked out.

"Baby girl, I didn't promise you shit," Radric said, coolly as he sat down on the bed, going through his text messages while smoking a Newport.

"Oh, you don't remember when I was on my knees sucking your dick, and between you oohing and aahing, you told me you'd give me that money so I could get caught up on some bills?"

"That shit don't count."

"Why not?"

"'Cause I was under duress. Shit, my dick was in your mouth. I didn't have no choice but to agree wit' whatever you said. You had me in a vulnerable predicament," Radric slightly smiled.

"Let's see how much you gon' be smiling when I call yo' girl and tell her you at the Ramada wit' me."

"Call her! Fuck, you can use my phone! I'll speak to her myself."

"Motherfucker, you ain't shit!"

"Damn right! And just like you know it, so do she."

Tierra grabbed her purse, pissed that she gave that nigga some pussy, again, when he hadn't hit her off with any money. But in reality, she would've fucked Radric regardless. She had been dealing with him off and on for over a year. Yeah, he had a girl, but so did just about every other nigga in these streets. But Tierra actually dug Radric. He was sexy as shit, and could fuck like no other. It just so happened that she was really hurting for the paper, and at the moment, had no time for free fucking. If Tierra had known Radric would be playing these types of games, she would've hit one of the low-level dudes around the way, who would've been throwing their dough to get down with a hood legend like Tierra, with no questions asked.

"Fuck you, Radric! I ain't got time for this shit tonight."

"Tierra, baby, where you going?"

"Don't 'baby' me. You got me over here begging you for chump change. Fuck that! I got moves to make."

"I thought you was riding wit' me to LaGuardia to pick my man up from the airport?"

Tierra crossed her arms in front of her chest and stared at Radric like he was smoking crack. "Nigga, I ain't going nowhere wit' you. Dude, I got bills to pay."

"Shut the fuck up wit' that silly shit. You know I got you. Here, take yo' five bills so we can go," he said, pulling out a wad of cash from his back pocket and peeling off five Benjamin Franklin's.

"Why you play so fuckin' much?" Tierra moaned, relieved but exasperated for having to go through all these changes to get money she desperately needed.

"'Cause I like seeing you get all worked up."

"Well, since I gave you your entertainment for the evening, you can pay me for that too," Tierra hissed, grabbing three more bills off the top of Radric's stash before he had a chance to put it back in his pocket.

He started to frown up, but before he could say anything, Tierra cut him off. "Let's just call us even now."

"Whatever! Let's go," Radric said, grabbing his car keys as they headed out.

On their drive to LaGuardia, Tierra sat back in Radric's Range Rover, thinking about how fucked up the last few weeks had been for her. She was living in an apartment she couldn't afford, and scrambling to make this month's rent. She had gotten the final cut-off notices for her electric and cable bills. She hadn't paid her car note in two months, and knew the repo man would be showing up at any minute trying to take her shit. That's why she had it stashed at one of her girlfriend's crib. Tierra couldn't understand how her life had taken such a drastic turn for the worse so quickly. It seemed like yesterday that money was flowing in every direction for the chocolate-brown beauty. And now, at the ripe age of twenty-one, the well seemed to be drying up.

"Yo, there my man go right there," Radric belted out, breaking Tierra out of her somber thoughts. He pulled his truck over at the American Airlines terminal, and Tierra instantly zoomed in on the tall, slender cat. As he walked closer to the truck, she had never seen a man with such a rich, smooth auburn complexion. It looked like you could glide your finger across his face and, it would feel like silk.

Radric jumped out the car and gave the dude a hug, showing mad love. "Man, it's good to see you."

"Likewise. Now, let me get in before one of these knuckleheads come over here telling us to fuckin' move."

Radric popped the trunk, and his friend threw his bags inside before getting in the backseat. "Renaldo, this is Tierra."

"Hey, nice to meet you," Tierra grinned.

"Nice to meet you too. But nigga, you need to stop playing. Only my mother calls me Renaldo. You can call me Renny."

"Got you."

"You gon' always be Renaldo to me," Radric joked.

"Whatever, so what we doing tonight?"

"What you wanna do?"

"It's on you, but I damn sure want something good to eat."

"Yo, I know this new spot where the food is on point. We can go there. You rolling wit' me?" Radric turned and asked Tierra.

"I don't know. There were a few things I needed to handle."

"It can wait. Call one of your girls up. She can come with us."

"You so damn bossy!"

"You know it!"

"I'll call Nichelle... nah scratch that, she got school in the morning."

"School? You 'bout to have my man on some jailbait shit," Radric teased.

"Nichelle got a man. Ain't nobody tryn'a hook her up wit' your people. I'll call Simone. She might wanna come." Tierra flipped open her cell phone and called her friend. Simone was always down for a free meal, especially one with a cutie like Renny.

The phone just rang, until finally she picked up. "Hello," Simone answered with an attitude.

"What's up? Everything a'ight?"

"My baby daddy trippin' and shit, but I'll be straight. What's up?"

"Nothing. I'm going out to dinner with Radric and his friend. Do you wanna roll with us?"

"Girl, yes! I need a good meal, and I know Radric ass gon' take us to a fly joint."

"Cool. So we'll pick you up in about an hour."

"Nah, I'll meet you there, 'cause I have to find a babysitter."

"Make sure you come, Simone."

"I got you. Trust me, I want that meal and a few drinks too. Text me the location."

"I'm on it," Tierra said, flipping her phone shut.

"So, is your girl coming or what?" Radric inquired.

"Yeah, she's gonna meet us there."

"There was no need to bring a friend for me. I'm good," Renny said, leaning back in the seat.

"I know you ain't hard up, nigga. I just wanted someone to entertain Tierra so she wouldn't be all up in our shit."

"Fuck you! I ain't got no problem going home! You can drop me off now."

"Yo' ole feisty ass always gotta get extra," Radric said, playfully tapping Tierra on the head.

"Whateva, nigga! Being feisty is the only flow you respect, and that's real talk," Tierra smacked, as she gave Radric the side-eye and glanced back at Renny.

Tierra did hope Simone would find a babysitter and meet them for dinner. Renny was too cute to pass up, and being that he was Radric's friend, he was off limits to her. She couldn't help but think that it would be a damn shame to let all that fineness go to waste.

"Damn, Radric, I thought you said this spot was on point!" Tierra popped, squeezing into the small booth at the hole in the wall restaurant.

"I said the *food* was on point...and it is," he said, signaling the one waitress over, who was working every table.

"It's always the raggedy spots like this that be having the killa food," Renny commented, cracking open the menu.

"No need for that," Radric said, grabbing the menus. "I'll be ordering for all of us." He handed the menus to the waitress. "And yo, where your friend at? Call and find out if she still coming. Ain't no sense in ordering her some food if she ain't gon' show up."

Right when Tierra was about to hit the talk button on her cell, Simone came busting through the door in an outfit more appropriate for a nightclub than a dingy restaurant. Tierra waved her hand, getting Simone's attention.

"Yo, I just knew you must've texted me the wrong address when the taxi pulled up to this spot," Simone said, sliding her slim figure in the seat next to Renny.

"Girl, I said the same thing when we walked up in this place. But Radric swear down this food is the truth."

"Shit, I wasted a good outfit and a babysitter for

this!" Simone complained, doing an intense stare down of the scene, until her eyes rested on the man sitting next to her. She had been so busy being disgusted with Radric's choice of restaurant, that she hadn't paid attention to the eye candy right in front of her. "And who might you be?"

"That's Renny," Tierra answered, before anybody else had a chance to say anything.

"Nice to meet you, Renny." Simone extended her hand, and at the same time gently kicked Tierra's leg under the table. Tierra smiled, knowing her friend's disappointment had quickly shifted after seeing what she could possibly have for dessert.

"Good to meet you too. For a minute we thought you wasn't gonna be able to make it."

"Luckily for me, I was able to," Simone said, casually licking her lips in Renny's direction.

"Oh, so you good on the restaurant now, huh, Simone? You wasn't saying that a minute ago."

"Radric, ain't no need for you to get testy. I don't have a problem admitting when I'm wrong. This place definitely has a lot more to offer than I originally thought," she said, giving Renny a flirtatious smile.

It was Tierra's turn to kick Simone's leg, and both women gave each other an undercover wink, which they knew meant, *Good looking out!*

In These
Streets

They say life is what you make it, and as Nichelle sat in her sixth period class, bored with listening to the English teacher, clearly she wasn't making much of hers. She stared at the clock on the wall, counting down each minute and waiting for the bell to ring so she could break out. Let's just say, scholar she was not, and she had no intentions of ever being one. Nichelle felt what they were teaching in class couldn't prepare her for the survival tactics necessary to exist in the streets.

Instead of using the hour to absorb knowledge from the books, Nichelle would reminisce back on the period in her life when she thought shit was sweet. This was in Charlotte, when she lived in a nice house with two parents. Money wasn't an issue, and her mother stayed in the mall, shopping all the time, and buying her new clothes and toys.

That quickly changed, like so many other things, after that fateful day. Their journey had led them from shacking with damn near complete strangers, to staying in homeless shelters, to finally planting roots in Queens, New York. Reliving that painful voyage kept a dark cloud of depression over Nichelle. The only way she found solace back then, was in her belief that somehow a better life awaited her, and one day that was exactly what happened.

"I'll see you all tomorrow, and don't forget your essay is due on Friday," the teacher told the class after the bell rang. Hearing that announcement instantly brought Nichelle out of her daydreaming.

"Nichelle, can I speak to you for a moment?"

"Sure. What is it, Mr. Chambers?" she asked, chewing on her watermelon flavored bubble gum.

"How's your essay coming along?" Mr. Chambers sat down on the edge of his desk and lowered his glasses to the tip of his nose, waiting for her response.

"It's coming," Nichelle answered, nonchalantly.

"Nichelle, you're on the verge of flunking this class. If you don't do well on this essay, you will no longer be on the verge... you will flunk."

"I got you. I'm almost done," she lied, knowing that she hadn't even written the first word."

"Excellent. I'm glad to hear it."

With that, Nichelle turned to walk away, anxious to bail on her uptight teacher.

"Oh, Nichelle," he called out before she had a chance to leave.

"Yes?" she turned her head around quickly to see what else the teacher had to say. That's when she caught him giving her ample ass that same lustful glare the boys in her high school did.

"If you need any help on your essay, please don't hesitate to ask. That's what I'm here for, to help my students," he added.

"I'll keep that in mind. But... umm... I need to be going," she said, dismissing her teacher as she walked out the classroom thinking one thing: *The lust of the flesh was the same for all men. Whether they were dope boys from around the way, or so-called upstanding men wearing a tie and slacks, they all had pussy on the brain.*

Nichelle had that opinion about all men, until she met and fell in love with Carmelo Clayton. Carmelo was the man who swooped in and gave her that better life she thought was out of her reach for so long. Before he came along, it was all about watching, and sometimes helping her girl, Tierra hustle dudes for whatever she could get. But that was no longer necessary, because Carmelo fulfilled all of Nichelle's needs. If Nichelle had her way, she would say, "Fuck school" and spend every minute of every day with him. But Carmelo insisted that she graduate and get a high school diploma, so that's what she intended to do.

Nichelle grinned as she walked out front to the school parking lot and saw Carmelo waiting in his regular spot to pick her up. She loved how all the females would be sizing up her man, wishing they were the ones sitting in the passenger side of his silver, chromed out Benz. Some of the chicks in her school truly had no shame. They would damn near throw the pussy at him. They would walk in front of his ride and act like their skirts were somehow accidentally being lifted up. But yet, they were panty-less, and all you saw was bush. Others would walk right up and knock on the driver's side window, handing him their digits. He would give them that million-dollar smile, and simply toss the paper on the ground.

"Watch where you going!" one of Carmelo's annoying admirers barked as she purposely bumped into Nichelle as she was walking to Carmelo's car.

"Lerrick, why don't you watch where you going, since you bumping into me, not the other way around."

"Ain't nobody doing shit to you. Please! She think she so damn cute," Lerrick hissed, to one of her friends as she brushed her shoulder against Nichelle.

"Oh, you dying for an ass whooping out here, ain't you, Lerrick?" Nichelle put her hand on her waist, letting her adversary know not to let the innocent face fool you.

"Baby, is everything a'ight?" Carmelo called out, stepping out of his Benz.

Both Nichelle and Lerrick turned in Carmelo's direction, and then back at each other.

"I'm straight, boo, unless Lerrick got something to say." Nichelle folded her arms and gave Lerrick the standoff look.

Lerrick rolled her eyes and went back to talking to her friend.

"Oh, that's what I thought." Nichelle tossed her hair in Lerrick's face as she turned and walked towards her man.

Lerrick and her friends stared in disdain as Carmelo greeted Nichelle with a hug and kiss, lifting her slightly off the ground. "That bitch make me sick!

But she gon' get hers one day, just wait and see," Lerrick seethed.

"What happened over there?" Carmelo asked, as they got in the car and he drove off.

"Hating ass ho's, that's all. Nothing you need to worry about, baby."

"Anything that involves you, I'm gon' always worry about," he said, reaching for Nichelle's hand.

"And that's why I love you, because you always got my back."

"And your front," he grinned.

Nichelle squeezed Carmelo's hand and smiled. To her, Carmelo was the best thing in her life. She would never forget the day she walked into the corner store over a year ago, as he was coming out. She had never seen a boy so cute in her entire life. His pecan complexion glistened in the sun. When he smiled at her, she was in awe of his perfectly straight teeth, mainly because she was wearing braces and was dying to get them taken off. Her long black hair was up in a ponytail, and she had some cut-off shorts and a tank top on. It was one of the hottest days of the summer, and she wanted to reach for the bottle water he was holding and pour it all over her body.

When Carmelo smiled at her, she couldn't help but smile back, and was immediately embarrassed by all the metal decorating her mouth. She knew for sure he was turned off and thought he was wondering why this awkward girl was all up in his face. But instead of walking away, he stopped and said, "Where you get those cat eyes from?"

"My grandmother. Yeah, I got them from my grandmother," she repeated, as if this was going to be the only time she had a chance to speak to the guy she decided she wanted to be the father of her children.

"Is your grandmother still alive?"

"Yes."

"Well, next time you speak to her, you need to thank her for blessing you with those pretty eyes."

"I will," Nichelle replied, knowing she would probably never speak to or see her grandmother, since her mother said in no way could they have any communication with people from their past life. But Nichelle continued to grin and nod her head at the stranger as if he had her in a trance. The funny thing was, before that moment, Nichelle never did like her grayish-green eyes, because she felt they made her look weird. But hearing the compliment from the man that she instantly had a crush on made her pop her eyes open even wider.

"Promise?"

Nichelle just nodded her head yes, as she begged the Man up above not to let this dude walk out her life. He must of heard her, because by some miracle when she came back out of the store, Carmelo was waiting for her, and they had been together ever since.

"Girl, Radric is on his way. Where yo' peoples at? We can't bring Lil' Anthony with us on our date," Tierra huffed, as she watched Simone change her son's dirty diaper.

"My cousin was supposed to been here like twenty minutes ago, and she ain't answering her cell or her home phone."

"Well, call yo' moms."

"She at work. She don't get off until late tonight."

"You betta call Big Anthony and tell him to get his ass over here and watch his son... shi-i-i-t!"

Simone stared at Tierra with her mouth frowned up, trying to determine if she was serious with the suggestion before responding. When Tierra didn't hesitate with her proposal, Simone responded, "We'd be better off wrapping the baby up and carrying him in my purse, 'cause ain't no way Ant gon' watch his son so I can go out ho-hopping wit' you."

Tierra sat down on the living room couch exasperated. "I can't believe this shit! I finally hook you up with a fine, rich nigga, and you 'bout to fuck up the game plan 'cause you can't get nobody to baby-sit. See, that's why I ain't got no damn kids, 'cause they ain't nothing but money blockers."

"Tierra, don't you think I want to go on this date bad as hell? I'm so tired of being broke. Ant barely wanna buy Pampers, but he still be sniffing around the pussy like he got it on lock. Being pregnant and then trying my hardest to lose this baby weight has had me out of commission for a minute. Ain't but so far some food stamps and a welfare check can get you every month. I need a nigga to start bringing some money up in this crib... immediately!"

"Shit, you preaching to the choir," Tierra said,

determined to make this group date happen. See, Tierra knew that if Simone clicked with Renny, that meant more group dates would follow. And the more she stayed up in Radric's face, the more chances she would have to get him to lace her pockets. In her mind, this set-up would be beneficial to all parties involved. The niggas would have easy access to pussy, and she and Simone would have easy access to their wallets.

"Hold up! I know exactly who to call. She always comes through for me," Tierra said, picking up her cell phone.

"What's up, girl," Nichelle said, quickly answering her best friend's call.

"What you doing?"

"About to go get something to eat with Carmelo. Why what's up?"

"I need for you to do me a huge favor."

"Sure, you know I got you."

"I need you to come over Simone's crib and watch Lil' Anthony."

"Okay, when?"

"Now."

"Now? But Carmelo just picked me up."

"Girl, you know I wouldn't be stressing you if it wasn't important."

Nichelle let out a deep sigh, knowing she could never say no to Tierra. "Okay, I'll have Carmelo drop me off."

"Thanks, lil' sis. I knew you wouldn't let me down. I'll see you shortly."

"What was that about?" Carmelo questioned,

seeing the distress on Nichelle's face after she finished her call.

"I'm sorry, baby, but I need you to drop me off at Simone's so I can baby-sit."

"Why the fuck you gotta baby-sit for Simone?"

"Tierra asked me to, and you know I can't tell her no."

"I don't see why not. Ever since I met you, you bend over backwards for that chick. I know that's your girl, but damn!"

"She's more than my girl...she family."

"Okay, I get that, but she got you babysitting her girl's kid! Come on now! It seems like she taking advantage of y'all's friendship."

"Nah, I'm mad cool wit' Simone too. Regardless, Tierra has done so much for me I could never feel like she's taking advantage of our friendship."

"You say that now, but everybody got a limit, and believe me, one day Tierra will push you to yours."

Nichelle heard what Carmelo was saying, but it didn't ring true to her. She had no limit when it came to her friendship with Tierra. When Nichelle and her mother finally got out of the homeless shelter and got housing in one of the projects in Queens, Tierra was the first person to befriend her in the complex. With Tierra being four years older than Nichelle, she became like the big sister she never had.

When her mom would have to work long hours, it would be Tierra who stayed with her. When girls in the neighborhood would try and bully her, it was Tierra who would step to them with balled fists and let them know it wasn't going down. And as Nichelle began blossoming into a young lady, it was Tierra who taught her how to style her hair, put on makeup, and even bought her clothes that Nichelle could never afford. Tierra could do no wrong in Nichelle's eyes.

She admired how Tierra seemed to have all the men chasing after her and would hustle them for their paper, something Nichelle never had the confidence to do. By the lustful stares dudes would constantly give her, Nichelle knew she wasn't a busted chick, but no matter how attractive she appeared on the outside, there was always that underlying feeling of insecurity she harbored inside. And that was what she admired most about Tierra—her confidence and generosity.

It was Tierra who used some of her trickin' money to get Nichelle the braces she desperately needed, but her mother couldn't afford. Kids would tease her so badly about her stacked teeth, that she would sometimes come home in tears. Tierra wasn't having none of that. At the time, she was messing around with some balling, out of control cat in Brooklyn, and she made him pay for everything. That was just the type of person Tierra was, and because of that, Nichelle would forever be loyal.

"You sure Nichelle is coming?" Simone asked, Tierra as they stood at the top of the stairs in front of her apartment building.

"Girl, yeah. You know Nichelle always got my

back."

"Well, what's taking her so long?"

"It ain't been that long, and who knows where they were coming from. They could be stuck in traffic or anything. But trust me, if Nichelle said she will be here, then it's as good as done."

"Oh shit, here come Radric and Renny now!" Simone said, first noticing the Range coming down the street."

Tierra walked down the stairs as Radric pulled his Range Rover to the curb. "Hey, fellas, we'll be ready to roll in a minute," she said, leaning her head inside the passenger side window.

"What we waiting on?" Radric questioned, in his typical inpatient voice.

"Nichelle."

"What, Nichelle coming too? We having some sort of orgy or something?" Radric joked.

"Nigga, shut up. She's coming over to watch the baby for Simone." Just then Tierra noticed the familiar Benz turning the corner. "Oh good, here she come now," she said, walking off.

Carmelo pulled up right behind Radric and parked his car.

"Hey, girl, I don't know what I would do without you," Tierra greeted Nichelle before she even stepped out of the car.

"You don't ever have to worry about that. I'm always here for you," Nichelle said, stepping out of the car and giving Tierra a hug.

"Hey, Carmelo," Tierra waved."

"Hi, Tierra," Carmelo responded dryly.

Tierra knew he wasn't a big fan of hers, but she honestly didn't care. She was happy that Nichelle found someone that genuinely seemed to care about her and had her back. But as far as Tierra was concerned, in her game book, men came and went, but *real* friendships withstood all the bullshit, and that's what she shared with Nichelle.

Nichelle and Tierra started walking towards the apartment, and Simone practically tossed the baby to Nichelle before they even made it to the stairs. "Girl, thank you! He's almost sleep, and I left some bottles in the refrigerator, and his Pampers and everything else you need is right on the table," Simone explained, as Nichelle patted the babies back while he lay on her shoulder.

Radric and Renny sat in the car watching the three ladies interacting, but Renny had his eyes on one lady in particular. "Yo, who's that chick?"

"Oh, that's jail bait."

"She don't look like jail bait to me," Renny commented, sizing up Nichelle's ample ass that he was visualizing seeing out of her jeans. Then when he caught a full glimpse of her face as she turned towards Tierra while cradling Simone's baby, he became even more drawn to her. She seemed so at ease and affectionate holding a child that wasn't even hers. It was as if she had a natural motherly instinct and innocence that Renny found utterly sexy.

"She ain't that young, but nobody you should waste your time with."

"Why is that?" Renny wanted to know.

"For one, she got a man, and from what I understand, they both in it strong."

"What that got to do wit' me?" he asked, glancing over at Carmelo, who was leaning against his Benz.

"You still the same selfish motherfucker you always been," Radric chuckled. "But seriously, there's a ton of pussy out here, and a rich, pretty boy like you can have any piece you want. Let them two lovebirds have each other."

"I got you, man. I'll leave that alone." That's what Renny said with his mouth, but his mind had another agenda. He had seen a lot, and done a lot handling his business in these streets. And besides pushing dope and making money, too many things didn't catch his attention. But when something did, he became completely fixated on owning it, whether that was cars, clothes, jewelry, homes or a woman, and his new fixation was Nichelle. Renny didn't know when or how, but he was determined to add her to his collection.

U Better Think Twice

When you play the game that many refer to as 'street life', you're always given choices. For a lucky few, those choices lead to the 'hood riches they crave, and for the rest, either a jail cell with their name written on it, or even worse, an early death sentence. Although the risks are clearly laid out, the seduction of the game always lures them in.

"Simone, you ready for tonight?" Tierra asked, as they sat in the pizza joint, waiting for their order.

"Where ya going?" Nichelle inquired, sipping on her Coke.

"Nowhere exciting, just hooking up with Radric and Renny...again," Simone huffed, not sounding the least bit enthused.

"Why you say it like that? I thought you were feeling Renny," Tierra smacked.

"*Was*—when I thought he was feeling me too."

"What makes you think he's not?" Tierra pried, not letting up.

"Come on now, Tierra. We have all been out a few times together, and that nigga hasn't so much as whispered shit in my direction."

"Maybe he's the private type and don't like to show no affection in front of people."

"Then why the fuck he ain't ask me to go on a date alone, without you and Radric?"

"Maybe he waiting for you to ask first."

"Bitch, please!" Simone rolled her eyes, knowing Tierra was reaching. "That nigga ain't feeling me. It's time for me to move on and try to scam another rich motherfucker."

"Don't give up yet, Simone. You a bad bitch. That nigga will come around. Just give it a little more time."

"Nah, it's time for me to hang it up. Have Nichelle go wit' you," Simone said, flinging her hand up in the air.

Nichelle had been so quiet as the ladies went back and forth, Tierra had almost forgotten she was there.

"Don't even go there, Tierra," Nichelle quickly said, seeing her friend eyeing her direction.

"Why not? It'll be fun. We haven't done our thing together in a minute. It will be like old times."

"Tierra, have you forgotten that I have a man? A man who will flip the fuck out if he finds out I'm going on a date with another dude?"

"You don't have to tell him shit. It ain't like you his wife."

"Maybe not yet, but we're getting very close to it."

Both ladies practically broke their necks making sure they heard Nichelle correctly.

"Umm, sweetie, I don't see no ring on your finger," Simone popped.

"Not yet, but I'm sure it's coming."

"You sounding awfully confident over there. What makes you think that?" Tierra wanted to know.

"Because last night, Carmelo said he wanted us to move in together."

"A-a-a-a-nd? a lot of niggas un told me the same shit, but as you can see, I'm still living alone. And some of them sorry motherfuckers be trying to move up in *my* shit, and don't wanna pay no bills. Please!" Tierra said, shaking her head.

"Well, he gave me a set of keys," Nichelle said, pulling them out of her purse, "To our new condo in Hunter View. He's showing it to me today so we can start picking out furniture to decorate." Both of the girls' mouths dropped.

"You talking about the same Hunter View in Long Island City?" Simone asked, completely stunned.

"Yep."

"Them shits is off the chain! They're those brand new glass and steel buildings. I knew Carmelo was making paper, but not like that!" Tierra said, unable to believe what she was hearing.

"I guess all those trips out of town have really paid off," Nichelle smiled.

"I guess so," Tierra mumbled.

As the waitress put their extra large cheese pizza on the table, Tierra continued to be perplexed. She didn't understand how Nichelle had managed to make such a come-up without even trying, and she was barely holding on to her shit while she was putting in work every damn day.

Tierra had a lot of love for Nichelle, but she didn't think she was ready to be wifed by any baller out in the streets. To her, Nichelle was a very pretty girl, but in a young, naïve looking way. She didn't have that "in your face" sex appeal that Tierra proudly flaunted. It was annoying her that she was supposed to be the "Head Bitch In Charge", but somehow, Nichelle had managed to one-up her.

"I'm happy for you, Nichelle," Tierra managed to say, trying to play off her discontent.

Simone frowned up her lip and rolled her eyes at Tierra's blatant lie.

"I knew you would be. So now you understand why I can't go with you on that date. Carmelo is the real deal. I can't ruin that."

"I feel you. I guess that leaves you, Simone."

"I told you I'm done wasting time wit' dude."

"Just do it this one last night. I really need some money, and every time we all go on a date together, Radric hits me off wit' some paper."

"You getting hit off wit' some paper, and I can't even get no dick. That's some lopsided shit right there."

"Simone, you know begging ain't my thing, but I will. A bitch is broke, and I need your assistance. I promise I'll make it up to you."

"You better! But I don't understand why you can't go on the date by yourself."

"Because, right now Radric is like a little kid who is so happy to be at the playground with his best

friend. He wants to include Renny in every fuckin'
thing he do. Hopefully, his excitement will die down
soon, and we can do our own thing without Renny
tagging along."

"Yeah, you better hope it happens real soon,
because just like you need to make some money, so
do I."

"Hey Ma," Nichelle called, opening the door to
her mother's bedroom.

"Hi, baby. I wasn't expecting you to be home so
early. I just knew you would be out with Carmelo."

"Yeah, he had some business to take care of.
Plus, I wanted to talk to you about something anyway."
Nichelle sat down next to her mother on the bed.

"Is everything okay?"

"Oh yeah, you can get that worried look off of
your face."

"Good. Now, tell me what's going on. You know
I have to get ready to go to my night job in a little
while."

"Then I better not beat around the bush. Carmelo
wants us to move in together."

Sheila continued getting her cleaning service
uniform out of the closet, not giving any reaction to
what Nichelle just said.

"Ma, did you hear me?"

"I heard you, but I don't know what you want
me to say. You can't possibly expect me to give my

approval. You're only seventeen, Nichelle."

"I know, but I'll be eighteen before you know it. I'm always with Carmelo anyway, and you're hardly ever home."

"Still, that ain't no reason for you to be shacking up with no man."

"But I thought you liked Carmelo."

"Liking Carmelo ain't got nothing to do with this."

"Then what is it?"

"I was your age when I left my mother's house and moved in with a man. It was the worst mistake of my life. The only good thing that came out of that was you, and…" Sheila's voice trailed off.

"Me, and what?"

"Nothing," Sheila said, not wanting to relive such a painful time in her life.

"Are you talking about my dad?"

"It doesn't matter, Nichelle. The point is, when you're young, you think with your heart and not your head. My mother never stopped me from doing what I wanted to do, and I'm not going to stop you."

"Are you saying I can move in with Carmelo?"

"What I'm saying is, you gon' do what you wanna do anyway. Because when you start laying down with a man, you become one with that man. So at this point, it don't even matter what I want, because you're going to do what he wants. I work three jobs, and I'm too tired to be chasing you around trying to tell you what to do."

"Ma, you know I care about what you want."

"That's probably true, but I guarantee you care

about what he wants more. I know this, because I've been where you're at right now. Just remember, you better think twice about the decision you're making. Because when you start acting grown, you get yourself caught up in grown people shit."

Nichelle sat there for a minute, digesting what her mother had said. She knew there could be some consequences moving in with Carmelo, but she was willing to take her chances. Carmelo represented the stability she desperately wanted since losing the man she considered to be her father at such a young age. She yearned to feel wanted and loved. That is what Carmelo gave her, and she wouldn't let anything or anyone keep them apart.

What's Really *Good*

For many who get a taste of being on top, they develop a compulsion that only money and material gain can soothe. When it seems to be slipping through their fingers, only then can you see how low they will go to hold on to it.

"Baby, I can't believe we're living together. You're the best thing that has ever happened to me." Nichelle turned over and kissed Carmelo as they lay in bed.

"I feel the same way about you."

"Really?"

"No doubt."

"Why do you love me?"

"Huh?" Carmelo asked, taken off guard by the question.

"Why do you love me? I mean, you can have any girl in Queens, or any other borough, so why me?"

"Why not you? Who wouldn't want to wake up to you every day, and go to sleep with you every night. Especially since you got those braces taken off," he teased.

"Shut up!" Nichelle said, hitting him with her pillow. "I'm being serious right now."

"Okay, I'll be serious too." Carmelo sat up and pulled Nichelle close to his chest, staring deeply in her eyes. I love your loyalty to Tierra, even though I don't feel she deserves it. But I know if you're that loyal to her, there is no limit with how far you would ride for me. I love how you care about how other people feel, and you put their needs first. I love how you don't even realize how special you truly are. But most of all, I love how you feel when I'm inside of you." Carmelo smiled, and began gently kissing Nichelle's lips. He then lifted her hair up, and showered her neck with soft but sturdy kisses. As his fingers caressed her hardened nipples, Nichelle laid back and her legs instantly opened, begging for the dick her body had begun to depend on.

"Baby, I hope you'll always love me," Nichelle whispered, between inviting moans.

"I will, until the day I die," Carmelo said, in a low voice as he entered her, hypnotizing Nichelle with his words and his manhood.

Tierra sat on the bed watching Radric smoke a blunt while he and Renny cursed out the Knicks for getting their asses kicked—again. She was tired of sitting in the hotel room, bored as shit, but leaving wasn't an option. She needed money, and she wasn't leaving until she got it.

"Baby, you wanna take a hit?" Radric extended his arm in her direction, holding the blunt.

"You go 'head, I'm good." Tierra didn't want anything fucking up her focus. She knew Radric had that powerful shit. She didn't want to take a chance of her brain becoming so mellow and lazy that she would forget to ask for that dough she needed.

"You looking all bored over there. Why don't you call one of your homegirls and have them come over to keep you company?" Radric suggested.

"I thought *you* were supposed to be doing that."

"I have to keep my man, Renny company. If you would've had Simone come with you, you wouldn't be complaining right now."

"I told you Simone was busy, and you know Nichelle's living with her man now, so she's on lock."

"Then I guess you better start looking for some new friends, or entertain yourself," Radric joked.

"Funny!" Tierra folded her arms and side-eyed Radric.

"Nichelle; that's the girl who came over a few weeks back to baby-sit for Simone," Renny casually inquired.

"Yep, that's her."

"Ain't she a little young to be moving in with a man?"

"I guess her mama and man don't think so, because they are for sure shacking up in a fly ass condo in Long Island City, playing house. I'm just waiting for her to tell me she's knocked up."

"What condo building is it?" Radric was

competitive when it came to what another baller had. He liked to try and figure out if the next man was racking in more cheddar than he was.

"Those new joints, Hunter View," Tierra informed him.

"Shi-i-i-t! Carmelo bringing in paper like that? Damn, I might need to holla' at that nigga about doing some business," Radric said, with astonishment in his voice.

"That was the same thing I said. But I've been to the crib, and this spot is hot. I mean, Manhattan skyline, top-of-the-line appliances and fixtures, including a washer and dryer. Fitness facility, motherfuckin' indoor parking, and to top it off, a private rooftop terrace with a gas grill. The shit is too tight."

"I need to step my game up. Shit, I thought you were the only one that was making money like that in Queens, Renny. Carmelo's out there grinding for real."

Renny remained silent, listening to Tierra and Radric go back and forth about how Carmelo was doing it big, and how Nichelle was benefiting from it. He found the conversation informative, especially since he hadn't forgotten about the young beauty who caught his eye many weeks ago.

"I wish I could stay, but I have some business to handle," Renny said, getting up from the chair.

"Man, you leaving already? But the game ain't even over," Radric complained.

"You know them niggas ain't coming back when they down by twenty. That game's over."

"True," Radric admitted.

"I'll get up wit' you tomorrow." Renny gave Radric a pound, while he stood up about to leave. "See you later, Tierra."

"Bye, Renny." Tierra was happy as hell that she finally got Radric alone so she could handle her business with him.

"Tierra, take your clothes off and get comfortable," Radric suggested as soon as Renny shut the door.

"I got you." Tierra unzipped her dark-grey leather snakeskin platform boots. She then slipped off her jeans and low-cut sweater, ready to service the man who would supply the cash she needed to get caught up on her rent and car note.

"Damn, your chocolate ass sexier than a motherfucker!" Radric said, smacking Tierra's ass, then squeezing it tightly with his hand. "Now kiss on my dick real good," he continued, unzipping his jeans.

"You know I can't wait to wrap my lips around your shit, but baby, I need you to do me a favor first."

"What's that, baby girl?" he asked, as he unclipped Tierra's lace bra and began pulling down her panties. "You know I need to see all that fine flesh when I'm fucking your mouth."

"No problem baby, just do me that favor."

"You still ain't told me what it is."

"I need two stacks to get caught up on my rent and car note."

"I got you. Just suck me off real good first."

Tierra quickly debated in her head whether she should get the cash first, or go ahead and suck his dick. She wanted the money in her hand now, but she felt

Radric was good for it. They had been fucking around long enough that she had no doubt he would cough up two thousand dollars.

"Lay back, baby, and relax. I'ma make you feel real good." And that's what Radric did. He continued smoking his blunt with one hand, and playing with Tierra's tits with the other as she got her deep throat on.

Tierra was working her tongue and mouth action like her life depended on it, and in her mind, it did. Her time had officially ran out. For all the designer shoes, purses and little trinkets she had piled up along the way from fucking with 'hood ballers, she was now totally cash broke. Radric was the only dude she was dealing with who could possibly hit her off with the money she needed. Because if he didn't, her only option was to go back home to the projects she had escaped from.

"Damn baby, you earning that dough! Suck that dick!" he moaned, pulling on the top of her hair.

Tierra took it all in stride, and continued on like a champion as she felt Radric's dick pulsating, ready to cum. She tried to pull her head away so he wouldn't bust off in her mouth, but Radric wasn't having it. He grabbed her hair even tighter and held her head still so she couldn't move. Next thing she knew, her mouth was full of nasty, tart tasting cum.

"Go 'head and swallow!" Radric demanded, still grasping her hair tightly.

Tierra had no choice but to ingest every drop. It was either that, or choke to death. She tried to look at it from the bright side; at least she would have the money needed to pay her bills.

"That, shit felt good, huh?" Tierra smiled.

"Damn sure did. That might be the best blowjob I ever had." Radric stood up and started taking off his clothes. "I need to take a shower, and then we can continue on to part two. I fucked your mouth, now I need some of that pussy."

"Sounds good to me. But, umm, can I get that money?" Tierra rubbed her fingers together, feeling that even if they didn't fuck, she had already earned her money.

"Oh yeah, let me get you that." Radric reached in his front pocket, turning his back. "Here you go," he said, handing some money to Tierra.

Tierra's mouth dropped, "This is only four hundred dollars! Where's the other sixteen-hundred I need?"

"Sorry, baby girl, but this is all I got."

"Radric, stop fuckin' playing wit' me! I know you got more money than this."

"Shit's a little slow right now. Be happy I gave you that."

"You let me suck your dick and bust your nasty cum in my mouth, and you talking this all you got? Come on, you have to do better than that."

"Tierra, I told you that's all I got," he stated firmly. "Now I'm taking a shower. You welcome to join me."

"I'll pass."

"A'ight, be lying in the bed when I get out."

Tierra was so pissed, her eye began twitching. She felt Radric had completely played her, but she wasn't letting him get away with it. After she heard him turn on the shower, she went over to his jeans and began searching his pockets. It didn't take long for her to see the wad of hundred dollar-bills bulging out of the back pocket. "This nigga ain't shit! He got all this bread and only wanna give me a measly four hundred dollars! Oh, I'll show his monkey ass what's really good."

She then noticed a small bag of dope in one of his other pockets, and decided to take that too and sell it to one of the corner dealers for some more cash.

"Bitch, what the fuck you doing? I know yo' trick ass ain't tryna rob me!"

Tierra was completely caught off guard and almost peed on herself. "Nah, your jeans fell on the floor and I was picking them up."

"You a fuckin' liar! Open up your hands."

"Stop trippin', Radric. I told you what happened."

Radric lunged at Tierra, grabbed her by the shoulders, and then forced her to open the palm of her hands. "I knew yo' ho ass was scandalous!" he yelled, looking at the money and drugs Tierra was holding.

Tierra didn't know what to say. She had literally been caught red-handed. "It's not what you think!"

"I don't let nobody steal from me, including my mama, let alone some 'hood ho." He grabbed the money and drugs out of Tierra's hand.

"Radric, you need to calm down."

"No, you need to get the fuck out before I catch

a case behind fuckin' wit' you." He let go of Tierra and began collecting all her shit.

"What are you doing?" Tierra was confused until Radric had all her shit in his hand, and then opened the door, tossing everything, from her clothes, shoes and purse, into the hotel hallway. "Nigga, is you crazy!"

"Yeah, for fuckin' wit' yo' ass!" he said, holding the door open. "Now, get the fuck out!"

"I can't leave, nigga. I ain't got no clothes on."

"I don't give a fuck!" He walked over to her, and before she could continue to plead her case, he lifted her body off the floor and tossed her in the hallway, butt naked.

Radric slammed the door in Tierra's face, leaving her to bang on the door, begging him to let her back in. But he could care less. He went into the bathroom and took his shower, erasing Tierra out of his mind for good.

Bad
Influence

There comes a time when all friendships are tested. When it climaxes to that point, it's as if the clock is ticking on a silent bomb that only each friend can hear in their head. And however the drama unfolds, it decides whether the clock stops and the friendship is kept intact, or if it explodes and all hell breaks loose.

"Yo, I'm so fucked up right now," Tierra said, as she pulled on a Newport.

Nichelle listened and watched in concern as her best friend's leg wouldn't stop shaking. "Tierra, calm down. It will all work out."

"Not this time. I'm so fucked. I need money! How did shit get so bad so quick?"

Between trying to console her friend, Nichelle was also stressing about the ashes that were conveniently falling from Tierra's cigarette onto the glass table, instead of into the empty soda can. "I'll be right back," she said, rushing off.

"Where are you going? Don't you see I need your full attention? Dang!" Tierra sighed.

Nichelle was trying to do just that, but she also

knew what a neat freak Carmelo was, and he would be pissed the fuck off to come home to cigarette fumes and ashes on the living room table.

"Use this," Nichelle suggested, putting a wide cup on the table.

"What's wrong with me using my can?"

"I think because the hole is a tad small so you're missing it, and all the ashes are dropping on the table. This cup is a lot bigger."

Tierra looked down at the glass table and clearly she was missing the mark. But she never liked to be told what to do, even when she was in the wrong. "Whatever!" she huffed, continuing to get her smoke on.

Nichelle picked up the can and wiped the table clean, then began spraying some clean linen scented Lysol.

"Is all that necessary?"

"Carmelo might be home any minute, and you know how funny he is."

"No, I don't. Why don't you tell me."

"Well…"

"I was joking, Nichelle! You don't have to explain Carmelo to me," Tierra said, cutting her off.

Nichelle didn't appreciate how short Tierra was being, but she excused it on the stress she was under. "Listen, I have a couple hundred dollars I could give you. Maybe that'll help."

"I appreciate the offer, Nichelle, but I need more than a couple hundred dollars. But, there might be a way you can help."

"Tell me what it is. You know I got you."

Tierra sat back and took a long pull off her cigarette before smashing it inside the cup. "I was thinking, maybe you can ask Carmello for the money. You know I'm good for it once I get back on my feet."

Nichelle swallowed hard, digesting the request of her best friend. Then out of habit, she pulled on her long ponytail, which she tended to do when nervous or unsure about something.

"Nichelle, what you nervous about?" Tierra asked, knowing all too well her friend's behavioral patterns.

"I'm not nervous."

"Yes the fuck you are. You always pull on your damn hair when you shook about some shit. It's just two grand, that's nothing for Carmelo."

"True, but how do I ask him for the money without pissing him off."

"Tell him my mom is sick, and that I need the money for some medical bills."

"You mean lie!"

"Nichelle, stop acting so fuckin' stupid. You have lied before."

"Yeah, but not to Carmelo."

"Look, this some serious shit. We vowed to always have each other's back. Wasn't I the one that would always defend you from the girls in the neighborhood tryna fight you? Wasn't I the one that would use my money to buy you fly gear, when yo' mama was trying to dress you in shit from the Salvation Army? Aren't I the one who is responsible for you having them straight ass teeth instead of the jacked up ones you were born with? Didn't I—"

"Okay, okay, okay! I owe you. I understand that. I'll ask Carmelo for the money, just…" before Nichelle could finish her sentence, she heard the door opening.

"Who the fuck been smoking in here?" were the first words out of Carmelo's mouth.

Nichelle walked quickly to the door ready to do damage control. "Hey, baby, sorry about that. Tierra had one cigarette. She a little stressed about her mom," she said, eyeing Tierra and already beginning the set-up for her money request.

"You know I don't like that shit. If she wanna smoke, she need to go on the balcony," Carmelo said, not even saying hi to Tierra, or even acknowledging her with as little as some eye contact.

"She will next time, baby." Nichelle gave Carmelo a brief kiss and then went back to sit down with Tierra as Carmelo went to the master bedroom.

"Good looking out. Now, I think you should go head and ask him for the loot," Tierra said, in a low tone.

"Now? I think I should wait until later on, after he's had time to relax."

"I don't have time to wait. Plus, you already put the plug in about my mom. You need to seize the opportunity while you got it."

"I don't know, Tierra. This might not be the right time."

"Just do it!" Tierra said, firmly. "It ain't gon' neva seem like the right time when you hittin' a nigga up for some bread."

Nichelle went ahead and amped herself up as

she got up from the couch and headed towards their bedroom.

Carmelo was lying on the bed with his hands folded behind his head, watching ESPN on the plasma television. He seemed so content, that Nichelle was reluctant to disturb him, but she knew that she would never hear the end of it from Tierra. "Hey baby, do you have a minute?"

"What's up?" Carmelo asked, not taking his eyes off the TV.

"Baby, something came up. Umm...an emergency, and I really need your help."

Only then did Carmelo's eyes divert from the TV and to Nichelle. "Are you a'ight, baby?"

She could see his eyes were full of concern. "No, it's not me. I'm fine. It's Tierra, well actually, Tierra's mother."

"What about her?" he questioned, nonchalantly.

"I don't know if I mentioned this to you, but Tierra's mom has been real sick."

"Nah, you ain't said nothing." Carmelo was now back to watching ESPN, clearly uninterested at what Nichelle was saying.

"Yeah, she's been real bad off. That's what got Tierra smoking and stressed out."

"Un-hun."

"The medical bills have been really pilling up and it's taken a really bad toll on their family," Nichelle continued, trying her best to plead her friend's fraudulent case. "I was hoping that maybe you could loan Tierra two thousand dollars to go towards paying off the bills."

Carmelo calmly picked up the remote control and turned off the TV. He then lifted up from the bed and met Nichelle's eyes with a sturdy stare. "I come home for a minute tryna get a little peace before I have to go hit the streets, and you hit me wit' this? Tierra put you up to this bullshit, didn't she?"

"What are you talking about? I told you her mother's been sick and I wanted to help them out, that's all. You know we grew up in the same projects, and they were always there for me, so I wanted to return the favor."

"I can't believe you looking me straight in the face and lying for that triflin' trick!" Carmelo stood up from the bed and walked away.

"Carmelo, where are you going?" she asked, feeling stupid as she followed behind him.

"Tierra, I need for you to get yo' shit and go!"

Tierra looked at Nichelle with a baffled expression, and then at Carmelo.

"Carmelo, what is wrong with you?" Nichelle knew she should've followed her first instincts, and talked to Carmelo about the money later when Tierra was gone.

"Yeah, Carmelo, what is wrong wit' you?" Tierra asked, with an attitude."

"Because your triflin' ass is nothing but a bad influence on Nichelle."

"Excuse me!" Tierra stood up with anger jumping out her eyes.

"You heard me. How the fuck you gon' have my

girl asking me for money to give to you? You ain't her pimp."

"Carmelo, stop! I told you that money was for Tierra's sick mother."

"Yo, if I was one of those niggas that beat women, I would smack the shit out of you for straight lying to me for this silly ass broad. This chick's mama ain't sick, and if she is, don't they got shit called Medicaid? Get the fuck outta here wit' that bullshit! What the fuck ya think I am, a lollipop? Because yah definitely tryna play a nigga like a sucka."

Nichelle had never seen Carmelo so angry at her before, and she didn't know what to say, so she remained silent. But of course that didn't stop Tierra from running off at the mouth.

"My mother is sick, and just because she lives in the projects don't mean she on Medicaid. Nichelle was only tryna help a sister out, just like I have done for her on many occasions. Who do you think was holding it down for her before you came along? It was me!"

"Yeah, and you always tryna dangle that shit over Nichelle's head. You the worse type of friend, 'cause *real* friends don't throw that shit up in your face every time they want something. They do it outta love, and keep it movin'. If yo' triflin' ass so hard up for cash, go get a motherfuckin' job. And one that requires more out of you than spreading your legs, 'cause you ain't getting no fuckin' handouts from me."

"Carmelo, that's enough!" Nichelle hated to see two people that were so important in her life going at it. She was caught between her best friend and her man, and hated every second of it.

"Don't worry about it, Nichelle. I was just leaving!" Tierra said, grabbing her purse. She brushed past Carmelo, wanting to spit in his face, but figured that action alone would break his "no beat on women" rule.

"I'm sorry, Tierra. I'll call you later on."

Tierra strolled past Nichelle not saying a word, and left, slamming the door shut.

"Carmelo, I can't believe you said all that cruel shit to her."

"Please, I know tricks like her. She's a snake. One day you gon' see that shit for yourself, and remember I warned you."

"Yo, where's homegirl at? For the last few weeks, every time I see you in the streets, she was posted up right next to you," Renny inquired, as he jumped in the passenger side of Radric's Range.

"I had to cut that bitch off."

"Why, what happened?"

"The whore tried to rob me for some money and drugs."

"Word? Why did she try to rob you? Wasn't you hitting her off?"

"Yeah, I was giving her a little something here and there. Then she came to me with some sad story. You know how ho's do. Talking about she need two stacks. I was like, a'ight shortie, I got you right after you suck my dick," Radric said, laughing about the shit. "Then after she finished, I tossed her a couple bucks, and when she thought I was in the shower, I caught her going through my pockets, tryna steal from me. Can you believe that broad?"

"Hell yeah, I can believe her! You was fuckin' homegirl on the regular. You couldn't hit her off wit' two stacks?"

"That ain't the point. It's *my* money, and I decide how I'ma spend it. These ho's in the streets need to recognize that their pussy is replaceable."

"Nigga, you crazy!"

As Radric drove over the Brooklyn Bridge, entering Manhattan, Renny was disappointed that Radric had cut off Tierra... for his own selfish reasons. She was his only connection to Nichelle. With her out of the picture, he had no way of knowing what moves she was making.

"What's up with your cousin, Arnez? He still going to hook you up wit' that new product?" Radric asked, kicking the images of Nichelle out of Renny's head.

"Supposed to be. He in Atlanta right now, but he'll be back in Philly in a few weeks, and I'ma meet him up there to test the shit out."

"Cool. I wanna roll wit' you when you do that."

"No problem. When I know for sure when I'm breaking out, I'll let you know."

"That works. So what, you've decided to stick around a little bit longer?"

'Damn, motherfucker! You tryna get me to

bounce already?"

"Renny, man, you know I like having you here, but I'm just surprised you staying. Originally you said you were coming for a couple of weeks to check on some shit you had set up. Those couple of weeks is turning into a couple of months, that's all. Don't you got peoples in ATL?"

"Besides my cousin, I ain't got nobody keeping me there. But right now, not only is there a drought in ATL, it's hot as a motherfucker. Feds locking up people left and right."

"Ooooh, so that's why you focusing on setting up shop here."

"I always handled business this way, but yeah, that's why I'm doing more, and ain't in no rush to bounce. But when shit cools down, I'll go back. Shit, you can ball all sorts of outrageous in ATL. But right now, that shit ain't a good look."

"So what happened down there?"

"Man, this chick Coco...have you ever met Coco?" Renny asked, not recalling if Radric had ever been around when he was handling business with one of his main connects.

"Nah, who that?"

"Coco is this Hershey chocolate bad ass bitch. She got a sister named Chanel, and for a minute, they were running shit heavy."

"Yo, I've heard of them. They twins, right?"

"Yep, that's them." Both men grinned. "Well, the Feds picked up Coco a few months ago, and were supposed to have locked up some of her workers too."

"What about her sister?"

"Last I heard, Chanel was still out. But they all are laying low, including Arnez. He been in Philly a lot handling some shit, so I don't know if he tryna set up shop there because of the shit poppin' off in ATL, or what."

"I feel you. Just don't bring that heat over here to Queens. Shit, we got a drought this way too," Radric chuckled, turning off the bridge.

"Man, I know. That same 'Operation Dry Spell' them motherfuckers had going on in Philly because of that large cocaine bust in the Caribbean on its way to the US, is expanding every fuckin' where. Quality cocaine is so scarce right now. Niggas stretching that shit out so fuckin' much, it's losing all the purity."

"Damn straight! That's why I'm tryna break bread wit' this new connect. I heard he got that gold."

"Who the fuck is that?"

"You know, that nigga, Marley's birthday party we hittin' up next Friday."

"Oh shit, I forgot all about that party. I thought he was just some nigga you was cool wit'. He got that prime coke?"

"Not him, but the nigga he get his drugs from. He supposed to introduce me to him at his birthday party."

"That's a party I think I might need to attend."

"Nigga, I told you to roll."

"Yeah, but I thought it was some regular merrymaking bullshit. Getting a connect to some prime product...that's a whole 'notha party in itself. So it's next Friday?"

"Yep, I'm heading to this spot now to get my suit."

"Suit, what the fuck, it's some baller, dress up shit?"

"Yeah, nigga, so pull out the arsenal."

"I'ma pull out more than that. If Arnez come through wit' his shit and this new connect work out, hell, the drought might be over before it really fuckin' started. And that's the type of news that keeps my dick hard, besides some fresh new, untapped pussy." Renny smiled, laying back in his seat, and feeling like luck was leaning in his favor.

It's Come To This

Many wonder if it's true that innocent children will have to suffer for the sins of their parents. If that was a proven fact, maybe more people would think twice about the path they take in life. I mean knowing that your little boy or girl, and even your unborn child, would have to carry the burden of your sins would motivate you to live your life differently...or maybe not.

"Damn Tierra, I can't believe you have to move out your apartment and back into yo' mama's crib. That's fucked up," Simone said, as she packed up the last box.

"*You* can't believe it? I'm still shaking my head over the bullshit. As broke as I am, I can't believe I lasted up in here this long."

"So what you gon' do with all your furniture?"

"My moms ain't got no room for it, and I can't even afford to put this shit in storage."

"Why don't you sell it?"

"'Cause I don't know who to sell it to, and I don't have time to try and find a willing buyer. I was supposed to been out of here two weeks ago, but I kept praying that I would luck up on some nigga to save the fuckin' day. As you can see, no such luck, and now I'm hauling ass tryna break out before I find my shit thrown out on the streets."

"Shit, I would love to have it."

"Are you tryna pay for it, or you asking me to give it to you?"

"I mean, shit, you ain't doing nothin' else wit' it! I mean, what...you gon' leave it here? You might as well give it to me." Simone was practically salivating at the idea of having the top-of-the-line Italian furniture replace the hand-me-down furniture her grandma gave her. If Tierra didn't give it to her voluntarily, she was contemplating having her baby daddy rob the joint after they left, but then it dawned on her that when Tierra came over to visit, she would see all her goods and know what was up.

"That ain't the point. This furniture cost a lot of fuckin' money. If you want it, you need to cough up some coins. If not, this shit can sit right here," Tierra snapped, rolling her eyes.

That's why yo' ass getting put the fuck out now...don't neva wanna share shit...selfish ass! Simone thought to herself. "How 'bout I make payments?"

"What, you mean like layaway? This ain't Wal-Mart."

"Tierra, do you wanna make some money off this shit or not?"

"Fine. How much can you give up now?"

"I can get my hands on about three."

"Three thousand?"

"Hell no!"

"Oh, 'cause I was about to say! Shit, if you can get a hold of that, then you can help me wit' some of these bills so I can stay up in my crib."

"No, three hundred."

"Three hundred! You need to come wit' more than that. This furniture cost thousands of dollars. That nigga, Lucci laced my crib right before he got locked up for that long ass bid." Tierra sat down on her couch and sulked. "That was when shit was sweet. If only I could rewind the time to back then."

"Well, you can't, so get over it. I might be able to come up with five hundred, if Ant gives me two."

"Shit, well you need to forget it, 'cause Ant ain't coming up wit' nothing."

"When he see this furniture, yes the hell he will."

"After you give me the five, how often are you going to make the payments, and for how much?"

"How much are you selling the shit to me for?"

"I can do thirty-five hundred."

"Girl, I'll be paying that shit off forever."

"Lucci paid over ten g's for it."

"And you paid nothing."

"Fine, I can do twenty-five."

"Make that an even two thousand, and I'll pay you two hundred dollars every week until it's paid off."

"Fine, but I want my five-hundred before you lift even a chair out this motherfucker." Tierra glanced around her spacious one bedroom loft, still trying to figure out how sugar went to shit overnight.

Nichelle sat in her English class, reminiscing on how fucked up the last week had been between her and Carmelo. Ever since the argument over Tierra happened, he had been giving Nichelle the silent treatment. Even when he would pick her up from school, no more than a few words were exchanged between them. The stress was taking a toll on her, because not only was Carmelo her man, but she considered him her best friend, right next to Tierra.

Then there was Tierra. She was salty at her too. It was as if Tierra blamed Nichelle for how Carmelo went at her, even though Nichelle felt she had put shit on the line for her friend. So the two people she felt the closest to were both throwing major shade her way, and Nichelle didn't know what to do to make it right. On top of all that, it was Nichelle's eighteenth birthday, and nobody seemed to remember or care.

"There's the bell. Class is now over. I'll see you guys on Monday. Have a good weekend," Mr. Chambers said, dismissing the students. "Nichelle, I need to speak with you for a minute."

Nichelle sucked her teeth, not in the mood for the drama. "Mr. Chambers, I know what you're gonna say. The paper I turned in late was some garbage, and I'm still gonna flunk your class." She sighed, as she looked down at the floor.

"Yes, your paper was late—scrape that—make that *very* late, but it was worth it."

"Excuse me?" Nichelle directed her eyes from the floor to meet Mr. Chambers' face. She needed to look directly in his eyes to make sure she heard every word he spoke.

"Your paper was worth the wait. To say I was moved by your story would be an understatement. The complex emotions of the young female character were incredibly profound. Nichelle, you're a very talented writer, and with proper guidance, there is no telling how far you can go."

"Oh, I see. I guess you're the one who is going to give me the proper guidance. What, you want some ass, is that it? I don't fuck for grades, Mr. Chambers, so if that's what you're looking for, you can go 'head and flunk me now."

She didn't fully grasp what she had just said to her teacher until she saw the horrendous expression on his face. But it was too late, she couldn't take it back. The silence in the room was eating Nichelle up. She didn't know if she should say nothing more and make her exit, and right when she decided that would be her best move, Mr. Chambers finally spoke.

"Nichelle, you are a very attractive young lady, but I would never jeopardize my career as a teacher by trying to have an inappropriate relationship with one of my students, or any student for that matter. If I have ever done anything to give you that impression, then I apologize. I genuinely believe you have a gift for writing. It doesn't have to be me, but hopefully you'll find someone to help you hone your craft, so you can take that gift wherever you want it to go in life."

"Are you trying to say you think I'm smart, Mr. Chambers?"

"Yes, you are smart."

"Nobody has ever told me that before. I guess it's easier for me to believe that you're like the typical man, running around with sex on the brain, than to think you see talent in me."

"Nichelle, talent is a gift that God gives to everyone. It is what that individual does with his or her gift that makes them stand out from everyone else. You can be like so many other people and let your talent perish, or you can be one of the chosen few who let it shine. It's up to you. I've done my part."

"And what is that?"

"Recognizing your talent and sharing that gift with you. You've been informed. If you decide to take advantage of your talent, I'll be here whenever you're ready."

"Thank you, but I better be going. My boyfriend is waiting for me."

"I understand. Have a good weekend."

"You too."

"By the way...Happy Birthday."

Nichelle turned her head towards Mr. Chambers and simply smiled before leaving his classroom.

With Carmelo still not saying more than a few words to Nichelle the entire ride home, she replayed her conversation with Mr. Chambers. For the first time in so long, her self-esteem got a boost. And this time it wasn't from some man making her feel cute or sexy, it was because somebody saw something that she never saw in herself—intelligence.

When Nichelle finally decided to write her paper, she sat for hours, unable to put down one word. It wasn't that her mind wasn't full of thoughts; it was that she was afraid to free those thoughts. But once she did, her words flowed and filled the papers. It was easy for Nichelle to relate to the young girl's emotions, because they were all hers too. To have somebody else, like her teacher, acknowledge how deep those feelings went, made the pain Nichelle struggled through to put them into words worthwhile.

"I knew yo' ass would be back up in here sooner or later. Hmph! You always complained this place wasn't good enough for you, but here you are."

"Ma, I don't need to hear this from you right now," Tierra gasped, as she placed some of her boxes against the wall in the hallway and tossed her bags into her old bedroom.

"Well, you gon' hear it. You and these fast ass girls always trying to find the easy way out. Messing around with these no good men who pushing drugs, killing off our own race...for what? So you can ride around in expensive cars that ain't yours, and wear some overpriced clothes that ain't even worth the fabric it was made from. You hard-headed women gotta learn the hard way."

"Can you save that preaching for somebody that cares, 'cause I don't."

"And that's why you back in this tiny ass apartment with me now, because you don't care about nobody but yourself."

"That's not true. I always tried to hit you off and help you out when I used to have money rolling in, but *you* didn't want none of it. That wasn't my fault."

"Why in the hell would I want some money you earned from laying on your back? I didn't raise you to be that way—greedy and materialistic. Even with you getting evicted from your apartment, car repossessed, not a dime to your name, you still can't see that money made the easy way don't never last."

"Trust me, wasn't nothing easy about how I got that money. I earned every cent, having to deal with the knuckleheads I came across. But yeah, right now I'm going through a tough time, but trust me, I'll be back on top of my game and out of your house."

Tierra's mother shook her head in disgust. "Child, this trife life that you living will catch up with you sooner or later. That I can guarantee you," she warned, pointing her finger at her daughter.

Tierra stared at her mother, undeterred by her words. She knew the woman who raised her meant well, but having money in her pocket meant more.

"Ma, I don't want to argue with you. I appreciate you letting me stay here until I get back on my feet. Can we please end it there? I have a lot of unpacking to do."

"I'm done. If you need some help, let me know.

And Tierra…"

"Yes?" Tierra sighed, feeling like her mother was about to go in for round 2.

"You're welcome to stay as long as you like. It may not be some expensive loft, but it will always be your home."

Tierra stood in the hallway holding her bag as she watched her mother disappear into the kitchen. She didn't know whether to be thankful by her mother's words, or scream out that this isn't the home or the life she envisioned for herself. And she never understood why her mother settled for this life either.

Growing up, Tierra always thought her mother was the embodiment of beauty. She had inherited her rich chocolate skin and the curves of a stallion. Tierra remembered men constantly coming at her mother hard, promising her everything, from fur coats to diamond rings, but she turned her nose on every last one of them. Her heart belonged to one man, and always would until the day she died.

Tierra never forgot the knock at the door that changed her life and that of her mothers' forever:

"Tierra, what dress do you think mommy should wear tonight? This silver one or this red one?" she asked, holding them both up for her daughter to see.

"Ummm, I think you should wear the red one. Daddy loves you in red."

"And how you know that?"

"Because I was with him when he picked out this dress for you. The only reason he bought you the silver one too was because he knows it's your favorite color, but he told me he hoped you would wear the red one, because that color made your pretty black skin shine even more."

"That's what your Daddy told you?" Tierra's mother smiled, thinking how lucky she was to have such a wonderful man in her life.

"Yes he did. He told me not to say nothing, but since you asked me, I had to tell you the truth," Tierra shrugged.

"That's right, and I'm glad you did. It's been decided. I'll be wearing this red number tonight. Your Daddy ain't gonna be able to keep his hands off of me. Maybe we'll make you a little brother or sister tonight."

"Yeah, I want a little sister, so I can boss her around and tell her what to do."

"I bet you do, with your grown self."

"I can't believe today is you and Daddy's one year anniversary."

"Neither can I. It seems like yesterday you were born, and now you're nine years old, we live in this beautiful new house, and I'm married to the man I've been in love with since I was in high school. Life is good, baby!"

"It sure is, Mommy," Tierra grinned, wrapping her arms around her mother's slender waist. "Mommy, was that the doorbell?" Tierra asked, as "The One I Gave My Heart" by Aaliyah dispensed from the radio.

"I don't know," she answered, turning the music down. Then she too her the doorbell ring. "Come on, let's go see who it is," she said, looking down at the watch her husband had given her as an early anniversary present. He told her it was only the first of many.

"You think Daddy forgot his key?"

"No. When he called a little while ago, he said he had one more stop to make, and he wouldn't be here for another hour." *But I wonder who it is,* she thought as she looked out the peephole. "Oh, it's Calvin."

"Uncle Calvin, what are you doing here? Did you bring me a present?" Tierra cheesed up, giving her father's best friend a hug.

"How is the prettiest little girl in all of New York? I don't have a present, but I did bring you something," he said, pulling out a hundred dollar bill and placing it in the palm of Tierra's hand. To Tierra, this was normal. All she knew was the good life.

"Calvin, I'm sorry, but Terrance isn't here. He should be home in about an hour. But then, we're heading out. Since you were his best man, you know it's our anniversary. He has some over-the-top night planned for us, as only Terrance can pull off. But you're welcome to come inside and wait for him."

Calvin stepped inside the spacious house and looked around. Every piece of furniture, wall décor to a simple light fixture, had Terrance's flamboyant touch to it. There was nothing simple about the man. He hustled hard in the streets, and lived life and spent money as if tomorrow wasn't promised, because he knew it wasn't, being in the drug profession.

"Calvin, sit down and relax. Tierra will entertain you while I get dressed. You know Terrance can't stand waiting. He's always late, but heaven forbid if somebody else is late."

"Nicole, can you come sit down with me?"

"I can't, I have to get ready for my husband," she blushed, loving to call her man that.

"Yeah, Uncle Calvin, my Mommy is putting on this red dress that Daddy bought her. She has to go get ready, because they gonna make me a little sister tonight."

"Tierra, hush your mouth! Calvin, I don't know what we're going to do with her. She is too grown."

"No I'm not. Daddy says I'm just smart."

"You are smart...so smart that I want you to do me a favor."

"What's that?"

"This guy who owed me some money handed me this envelope, but I was in such a rush I didn't have time to count it."

"No problem, Uncle Calvin, I'll count it for you."

"Do that, and make sure you write down the exact amount."

"I will," Tierra said, with excitement in her voice as she grabbed the envelope and hurried upstairs to her bedroom.

"Calvin, what's going on?" Nicole asked, feeling uneasy.

"Come sit down."

"I don't want to sit down. I want to know what is going on." Calvin sat there, stoic. "Hold up! I know you ain't over here about to tell me some ole' soap opera bullshit, like my husband ain't coming home because he's leaving me for some other heffa," Nicole popped, with crossed arms.

"Never that. You know you were the love of his life."

"Were?" Nicole murmured, holding her hand against her chest while the other one gripped her waist as his words sank in. She then started shaking her head from side to side as tears filled her eyes. "Not today! Not this! Not Terrance! Not my husband! Oh God, *no!*" Nicole's voice was so low, but anguish and grief screamed loudly from her face.

"Nicole, I'm sorry."

"How… what happened?"

"He was leaving the jewelry store, picking up a necklace he had specially made for you. He planned on giving it to you tonight. But some punk ass, low level dealer who knew Terrance was making paper, tried to rob him. Of course, Terrance wasn't gonna let that shit happen. He pulled out his gun and shot the nigga. But the nigga's partner, who had been waiting in the car, ran up on Terrance and blasted him. I still can't believe he's gone." Calvin put his head down in astonishment.

"What happened to the son of a bitches responsible for this?"

"The one Terrance shot died at the scene, and the other one was caught when he was trying to drive off. Luckily, somebody in the jewelry store saw what was going on and had called the police."

"Why did Terrance have to be so damn stupid? He should'a just given the man the necklace! This shit don't mean nothing! It's only material bullshit!" Nicole exploded, ripping off the platinum and diamond watch she was wearing. Then picking up anything she could get her hands on, from a vase to a lamp to the crystal plates on the dining room table, she began throwing them across the room.

Calvin wanted to stop her, but Nicole was storming through each room like a category 5 hurricane. All he could do was take cover until her rampage came to a halt.

"Mommy, what are you doing? What's going on? You're destroying the house!" Tierra yelled, as she ran down the stairs.

But her mother ignored her. She was so caught up in her own rage that it was as if Tierra was invisible and inaudible.

"Tierra, your mother is upset right now. Go back upstairs until she calms down."

"Uncle Calvin, I don't want to go upstairs! What's wrong with my Mommy? Why is she acting like this?"

Calvin held Tierra tightly, but her willpower was too strong as she broke free from his clutches and ran towards her mother.

Nicole had just picked up a beautifully detailed crystal and 24k gold frame, with a picture of her and Terrance holding Tierra at her Christening. Right when she was about to smash it against the wall like so many other objects she got a hold of, Tierra ran up to her with fear and anger in her eyes.

"What's wrong with you!" Tierra screeched so loudly that it could've cracked every mirror in the house.

It was at that moment that reality kicked in for Nicole. She realized that even though the love of her life was now dead, they shared a daughter who would now need her more than ever.

"Baby, I'm so sorry," Nicole finally said, as she stared at the picture she was about to destroy. The memory of how happy she and Terrance were that day brought a moment of calmness to her heart that she desperately needed.

"Mommy, what happened to Daddy? Only he can make you this upset." A single tear rolled down Tierra's cheek, and Calvin turned his head, not wanting to succumb to his own need to break down and cry.

"Baby, Daddy's gone. He's not coming back. The world couldn't handle a man like your father. He's gone to a much better place," Nicole sniffled, trying to hold it together.

"I want to go to that place too, Mommy," Tierra cried as she laid her head on her mother's stomach.

"So do I, baby... so do I."

Reflecting back to that day flooded Tierra with so many emotions, she almost lost her balance standing in the hallway. Not only did she lose her father that day, but part of her mother died with him. It was as if her mother lost all interest in love and life. They moved out of their beautiful home, and eventually ended up living in the projects in Queens. Although Calvin and some of the other dealers who ran with her father wanted to help Nicole out, she refused. She now looked at all profits made from pushing drugs as blood money, the same money that took her husband away. Nicole rationalized that if Terrance hadn't been a drug dealer making all that money, he wouldn't have been targeted, and would still be alive.

Tierra understood her mother's pain, because she too was in pain, but at the same time, she wanted her old life back... a life that was full of expensive cars, nice clothes and never having to worry about money. That was the life her father showed her, and that was the life she felt entitled to.

Because her mother had deprived herself of living a lavish life out of some sort of commemoration to her dead husband was beyond Tierra's comprehension. She felt her father would instead want them to live life to the fullest, like he always did. So as Tierra got older, she decided to do just that. She hustled men like her father hustled drugs, but yet it had come to this...back at her Mama's crib. It didn't matter though, because Tierra had the same determination as her father, and she would once again rise to the top.

Proposition

Everything has a price. Whether it is the designer stiletto boots that you can't afford, but yet they keep calling your name, or the trendy Gucci purse you spent two month's worth of rent on, only for it to go out of fashion before being able to fully floss in front of the ghetto-fabulous 'hood patrol. So, what's the price of ones' soul? No one knows until they put it up for sale.

It had been a week, and Nichelle still wasn't getting any love from Carmelo. She knew he could hold a grudge, but at this point, the shit was getting ridiculous. As she stood in the kitchen washing dishes, she thought about how nobody besides her teacher and mother had wished her a happy birthday. Nichelle didn't even mention how hurt she was to Carmelo, because she felt it would turn into an argument, and that was the last thing she wanted. But her frustration was reaching a boiling point, and she didn't know if she could stand another weekend of this madness.

As she contemplated what her next move should be, she heard Carmelo opening the front door. She decided it was time for war, and turned off the faucet, then dried her hands. Nichelle knew she had to confront her man now, before she lost her nerve and continued to remain silent.

"Carmelo, I need to talk to you about something," she said passively, greeting him at the front door.

"Can it wait until after I give you something?"

"Sure." Carmelo handed Nichelle a garment bag. "What's this?" she asked, unzipping it. "Oh my goodness! This is a Zac Posen gown!" Nichelle was in disbelief. She had only seen dresses like this in magazines, decorating famous celebrities, never up close, let alone holding one. She slowly pulled the dress out of the bag and let her hand glide across the lush fabric. It definitely didn't feel like the rayon and polyester blends she had grown to adore.

"You like it?"

"Fuck like! I love it! I can't believe you bought this for me. I don't even know a place to wear a dress like this."

"I do."

Nichelle looked at Carmelo with confusion written on her face.

"We're going to my man's birthday party tonight, and I want you to wear that dress."

For a quick second, Nichelle wanted to mention how he had forgotten her birthday, but decided not to be a mood killer. "Okay, but I need you to take me to the store because I don't have any shoes."

"Don't you see this other bag in my hand? I got you covered."

"Baby, thank you. I know you were upset with

me because of the whole Tierra fiasco, but I hope that's now behind us."

"It is. You're my baby, and I'm going to give you a night you'll never forget."

"I went from shopping at Saks, to rummaging through the sales rack in Rainbow. Ain't this some bullshit?" Tierra complained, as she and Simone tried desperately to find a dress that was cheap, but didn't look like it.

"What you think about this one?" Simone asked, holding a bright orange strapless dress under her neck.

"Trick, you know damn well if you gon' wear a cheap dress, you can't get it in no Easter orange. You need to stick to basic colors, like black and gray."

"But those colors don't do nothing for my skin tone. I like bright colors so I can stand out."

"Whatever, Simone. If you wanna walk up in that party looking like a reject Easter bunny, then go the fuck head and wear that whack ass dress."

Simone grunted and then immediately put the dress back on the rack. "Well, I don't see nothing in here. Let's go to Forever 21. They might have something cute. But we need to hurry up, because the party starts in a couple of hours."

"Wait, this right here is cute," Tierra said, picking up a short black dress with a plunging neckline. "I could jazz this up with those black and silver Gucci stilettos I have, and those diamond earrings."

"You talking about them diamond earrings that nigga, Keondre gave to you?"

"Yep."

"I thought you took them to the pawn shop."

"I did, but them crooked ass motherfuckers was tryna' bullshit me on the price. I know what the fuck those earrings cost. I was there when he bought the shit. They tried to play me like my shit wasn't official. I told those slimy bastards to kiss my ass and I kept my shit."

"Hell, I don't blame you, and with your current predicament, ain't no telling when or if a nigga will ever drop some jewels on you like that again."

"Thanks for the pep talk, Simone. After those words of encouragement, you got me feeling real optimistic," Tierra cracked, rolling her eyes. "Come on, let me pay for this dress so we can break out. All these bargain basement prices is giving me a migraine."

Nichelle twirled around in front of the mirror in amazement. Her teal, silk beaded chiffon dress with a thigh-high side slit made her feel like a 'hood goddess. No one would believe she was the same awkward, braces-wearing chick from the projects. She only wished that Tierra was there to see how nicely she cleaned up. This was just the sort of slap-you-in-your-face dress that Tierra would rock and shut the game down in.

"Damn, you look good!" Carmelo proclaimed,

snapping Nichelle out of her daydreaming.

"I still can't believe this is me."

Carmelo walked over to her and cupped her ample ass, "Yeah, it's you," he grinned. Don't nobody got a booty like my baby."

"Shut up," Nichelle laughed, placing a playful kiss on his lips.

"You ready?"

"Almost. Why, are we running late?"

"Nope, I just want to show you something before we leave."

"Let me touch up my hair and makeup, then we can go."

"Cool, I'll be in the living room."

Nichelle stared at her reflection in the mirror and knew nothing needed to be touched. She only wanted another opportunity to admire how she looked, not knowing if she'd ever feel this beautiful again. She grabbed her metallic hard-frame clutch, excited about the rest of her evening.

With Carmelo in his tailored smoky-gray Armani suit with a teal tie—the exact same color as Nichelle's dress—the duo exuded the style of a power couple. As they made their exit, during the entire elevator ride down they held hands, gazing into each other's eyes like a newlywed couple.

"If I forget to tell you later on, thank you for making this the best night of my life," Nichelle said, as they walked through the underground garage towards Carmelo's car.

"Wow, if you're saying that now, wait till you see

this."

"See what?" Nichelle turned her head in the direction that Carmelo was staring in. "Happy belated birthday, baby!"

Nichelle let go of Carmelo's hand and covered her mouth in amazement. There was a big red ribbon on top of an ice-blue CLS550 Mercedes Benz. "This can't be mine!"

"Yes, it can and it is. You deserve it, baby."

"And I thought you forgot."

"Of course not. The custom rims weren't ready on your birthday, so I decided to wait. I felt you would forgive me once you saw the present I had for you."

Nichelle was damn near speechless as she walked slowly, circling the car and taking in every detail. "This is really my car?"

"Now it is," Carmelo replied, tossing the car keys at Nichelle. She caught them, and her hands began shaking from her excitement. "So, are you taking me for a ride or what?"

"Carmelo, you really are too good for me. I don't know what I did to deserve you. Nobody has ever made me feel so special." Tears began rolling down Nichelle's face.

"Baby, don't cry." Carmelo gently wiped her cheek. "I'm not too good for you. We're perfect for each other. So stop with this Hallmark moment and drive us to this fuckin' party so you can show these 'hood rats how it's really going down."

"Yo, I see some serious heavyweight motherfuckers up in this joint tonight," Simone said, to Tierra as they both put an extra swagger in their walk.

"You ain't lying. One of these niggas got to be able to get me out my mama's house and back into the lifestyle I'm accustomed to."

"What about dude standing over there by the bar eyeing the shit out of you?"

"I know you ain't talking about that clear wrap over there!" Tierra barked.

"What, you don't fuck wit' white boys?"

"Hell no! You ain't neva seen me wit' one of those."

"Shit, if the motherfucker got paper why does it matter?"

"Besides the fact that no matter how bad they be irking my nerves, I love me some black men. A white boy gon' eventually say something out of pocket, and I'll have to slit his ass with my knife."

"Say something like what?"

"Call me a nigga, a black bitch...one of those terms that motherfuckers toss around loosely when they pissed the fuck off. 'Cause I know when I'm mad, I'm quick to start throwing around a race, color, or something to describe what you are. Even though I don't like it, it's one thing for my own to call me out my name, but when somebody of another race do it, you better call 911, 'cause it's about to go down."

"Girl, you crazy."

"No, I'm fuckin' serious. There are a lot of cute white boys running around, but they can bypass me and kick it wit' the cute little white girls out here…and there's no shortage of them."

"Speaking of cute, check out that fine specimen that just entered the building."

"You ain't lying! That nigga look fine *and* rich. Do you see that suit he got on? That ain't no S&K Menswear type bullshit either, his shit is official," Tierra commented, sizing the man up. Upon further inspection, her admiration quickly turned to disgust. "I can't believe this shit!"

"What?" Simone questioned while plotting on how to get the attention of the man who had walked in."

"When he turns his face back around, zoom in for a closer look."

Both women stood for what seemed like a few long minutes but were actually seconds, waiting to catch another full frontal glimpse.

"Get the fuck outta here! That's Carmelo! And look. Nichelle is with him, wearing a bad ass dress. She definitely didn't get that from Rainbow."

"Shut up, Simone!"

"I'm just saying…damn! But you can't front, Nichelle do look stunning."

Tierra watched as her best friend and her man made their way to the VIP area. She was burning up on the inside, wondering how in the fuck Nichelle's star was on the rise and hers was quickly fading out.

"Girl, come on, let's go over there and talk to Nichelle."

"You go 'head. I'ma stay over here."

"Tierra, she over in VIP. You know they gon' be poppin' bottles. And all the real ballers gon' be laying in the cut over there. I thought you said you wanted to get out yo' mama's crib. So come on, let's go." Simone grabbed Tierra's arm and guided her to the velvet rope.

When they walked up, the big burly security man was blocking their path and seemed to have no intention of moving out the way to let them through.

"Excuse me, but can you move? Our friends are waiting for us over there," Simone said, pointing in the direction of Nichelle and Carmelo, although their backs were turned away from them.

"You don't have a VIP wristband, so you can't get through."

"Come on, Simone. It ain't that serious. Let's go."

"Hold on a minute." Simone was adamant about getting to the other side of that rope, and a little thing like a three hundred pound man wasn't going to stop her. She began waving her hands and calling out Nichelle's name until she finally got her attention.

"Baby, I'll be right back. There's Simone and Tierra."

Carmelo glared in their direction and wanted to tell Nichelle to leave those money thirsty broads right where they were at, but didn't want to ruin her night.

"A'ight, baby."

"Hey, ladies! I'm so glad to see you!" After

security moved to the side, Nichelle gave Simone and Tierra a hug. She was sincerely happy to see her friends, especially Tierra.

"Nichelle, you killin' the game wit' that dress you rockin'. Drop a name. I know that's some label shit," Simone said, sounding hyped.

"Yeah, it's actually a Zac Posen. Carmelo picked it out for me."

"Bitch, you doing the damn thing," Simone added, giving her a pound.

"Yeah, that dress is hot," Tierra said, dryly.

"Come have a seat at our booth. I know you ladies want some bubbly."

"See, I told you." Simone nudged Tierra as they followed behind Nichelle.

When they sat down, Simone spoke to Carmelo, giving him a big Kool-Aid smile, but Tierra kept her face lowered, purposely not wanting to make eye contact with him.

"Let me pour you some champagne," Nichelle offered, trying to ease what could easily become a tense situation. Both the ladies raised their glasses up, ready to catch a buzz.

"Nichelle, come here for a second. I want to introduce you to somebody." Nichelle handed the bottle to Tierra and walked over to Carmelo. "Baby, this is Marley, the birthday boy."

"Hi, it's nice to meet you, and happy birthday."

"Nice to meet you too. If you don't mind, can I borrow your man for a moment? I want to introduce him to some of my people."

"That's fine."

"I won't be gone that long," Carmelo said, giving Nichelle a quick kiss on the lips.

"Man, that's a pretty little young thang you got right there," Marley remarked after Nichelle sat down.

"Yeah, that's my baby. She's the one."

"Let me find out you might be in love!"

"Ain't no might to it. I *am* in love."

"Ain't nothing wrong wit' that. Shit, I'm in love too...wit' pussy!" Marley said, slapping Carmelo on his shoulder. "But let's talk about my other love right now."

"Which is?"

"Money, nigga!"

"And I thought it was all pleasure tonight, no business."

"Always business, which brings pleasure." Marley grinned then added a wink. "I have this cat I've known for many years now, who is interested in getting his product from you. I told him you got the purist coke in the streets."

"So, I take it your vouching for him?" Carmelo wanted to make it clear before going any further. He didn't like fucking with new buyers, but since he knew Marley was a straight shooter and they had an excellent business relationship, he was willing to be open to the idea.

"No doubt. You know me, I wouldn't waste your time if I couldn't vouch for the nigga. He shoots straight from the hip, just like me."

"Enough said, lead the way."

"Radric, this my man, Carmelo."

"I've heard great things about you in the streets, but it's good to finally meet you," Radric stated as he stood up to shake Carmelo's hand. "This here is my partner, Renny." Renny rose up and shook Carmelo's hand too. "We're looking forward to breaking bread wit' you, so what you need to know?"

"Nothing," Carmelo answered in a composed tone.

Radric and Renny glanced at each other, then at Marley, who also seemed to be taken aback by Carmelo's one word response. "If you're good with Marley, then you're good with me. Let Marley know how much weight you want, and he'll give you the price."

The three men all exhaled in relief. "Thank you, we appreciate that. We hope to do a lot of business wit' you," Radric said, shaking Carmelo's hand one more time.

"Not a problem. Now, if you fellas excuse me, I don't want to keep my woman waiting any longer."

"Shit, I wouldn't either if my woman looked like that," Marley said, once Carmelo was out of earshot.

"You ain't lying! Nichelle definitely ain't looking like jailbait no more," Radric admitted.

"Her two friends are cute too," Marley said, noticing them for the first time.

"Yeah, but them two tricks is trash. You flash enough money, they'll be more than willing to spread 'em."

"Thanks for the inside scoop, Radric."

"You look out for me, I look out for you. That's what niggas making money together do."

"No doubt."

Renny sat back in his seat quietly, as Radric and Marley made small talk. He was interested in watching the interaction between Carmelo and Nichelle. He hadn't seen her in so long, and she was even more striking than he remembered. He didn't know if it was because she was dressed up or what. All he knew was that he wanted her for himself.

"Oh, baby, I love being inside my pussy!" Carmelo moaned as they made love in the living room in front of the fireplace. This was the third time they had sex since coming home from the party. Each time seemed to become more intense as their bodies and souls intertwined.

"Carmelo, I'm gonna love you 'til the day I die."

"You better," he whispered in Nichelle's ear, right before cumming inside her.

Right after a cab dropped Tierra off in front of the projects, she noticed a dark car driving slowly behind her. She started to pick up her pace, and the car began speeding up. She was about to take off her heels and make a run for it, but it was too late.

The driver pulled up on the curb, blocking her path, and flashed the high beam lights, flooding her vision. The driver then turned off the lights, and Tierra was able to get a clear look at the familiar face. "I have a proposition for you. Are you interested?"

"Yeah, I'm interested."

"Then get in the car."

Tierra walked around to the passenger side and did just that. In her mind, any proposition had to be better than the ones she currently had…which were none.

Ready For Whatever

When you're running the streets and living your life, it's easy to get so caught up, to the point, that not only do you miss the simple clues pointing to your fate, but also the ones slapping you right in the face.

"Girl, what time we going out tonight?" Tierra asked Simone as she sat on her bedroom floor giving herself a pedicure.

"Sorry, I have to pass. I have a date tonight."

"Wit' who?"

"You don't know him. It's a new cat I met."

"Met where?"

"At that birthday party we went to a few weeks ago."

"Who?"

"Just a guy," Simone answered, trying to keep it vague.

"So you not gon' give me no names, no details?"

"This nigga might be the one, so I'ma keep shit to myself for now. You know, I ain't tryna jinx the shit. If it go to the next level, *then* I'll fill you in."

"Let me find out you getting brand new. Humph!

If you knew what I know, you'd fill me in. I would hate for you to get sprung out and then realize you got stuck wit' one of my leftovers."

"Bitch, please! Trust, this is one nigga that ain't ran up in your pussy, that's why I'm keeping him to myself."

"You sounding real confident over there."

"I am. But like I said, if shit start getting serious, maybe we can go on a double date. He got a lot of niggas that work up under him. I'm sure one of them wouldn't mind kickin' it wit' you."

Tierra frowned at the phone, "Trick, you play too much. You know I don't fuck down."

"Damn, we are in a recession! I thought you was willing to take whatever you can get at this point."

"Don't worry about me, I'm good. You ain't the only one that came across some potential options. But I'll keep my shit close to the vest too. Girl, anyway, let me hit you back. That's Nichelle on the other line."

"Cool. Tell her I said what's up."

Tierra didn't even bother to respond and clicked over to the other line. "Hey girl, what's going on wit' you tonight?"

"Nothing. I'ma stay home and chill."

"I thought you, me and Simone could go out to dinner or something, but she got a date. So why don't we go catch a bite to eat? We haven't hung out in a minute."

"True, but I'm a little tired. Plus, I'm doing some writing."

"Writing? What sort of writing?"

"Like a short story. I'm actually enjoying it."

"Let me find out you 'bout to get all higher learning on me."

"Girl, be quiet."

"Well, can't you put your pen and pad down for a few hours and make time for your best friend? I mean, we *are* still best friends, aren't we?

"Of course! I am hungry, and Carmelo did say he would be home late."

"Then let's do it."

"Okay, I'll meet you in front of your crib in about an hour."

"Cool, I'll see you then."

"Man, shit been looking real sweet for the last few weeks," Radric said, between pulls from his blunt, while taking the ramp onto I-95 South toward the Turnpike.

"You right. Hooking up wit' that dude, Carmelo, was a very smart look. I ain't got no complaints about his product. Niggas everywhere loving that shit."

"And then we gon' get that heroin from your cousin, Arnez. Before you know it, we'll have the streets on lock. We'll be the one-stop shop that everybody wanna get they drugs from."

"That's the game plan. Shit, at this point, I'm fuckin' happy that Arnez finally decided to come out of hiding."

"What, the nigga on the run?"

"Fuck if I know. I didn't want to ask him too many questions on the phone. All I know is dude been missing in action since CoCo got locked up. Maybe that nigga was on the indictment too, and he just ain't wanna tell me."

"Yo, you think it's a good idea for us to be going to Philly and meeting up wit' him?" Radric asked, starting to feel somewhat paranoid.

"Nah, we straight. Trust, if that nigga thought for one moment some shit was going down, he would be the first to break the fuck out. That motherfucker values his freedom. He ain't tryna be locked up, not even for a day."

"Cool, 'cause I definitely wanna talk business wit' the nigga. I'm pumped that you let me roll wit' you down there."

"No doubt. You put me down wit' your connect, so it's only right I return the favor."

"That's what's up. Here, take a hit." Radric extended the blunt to Renny.

"No, I'm good," Renny said, declining his offer. And Renny *was* good. He never dabbled in any sort of drugs, only occasionally having a drink. He had constant paranoia about getting caught slipping in the streets from some sort of drug or liquor induced high.

"Suit yourself. That means more for me," Radric bopped his head to the music, as he sped down the highway.

When Nichelle pulled up in front of the projects that she grew up in, the whole block seemed to pause. All you saw was mouths dropping, and ooh's and aah's coming from corner watchers.

At first, Tierra thought everybody was sweating how her jeans were gripping her spectacular signature ass. But then as she looked forward and peeped the custom ice-blue CLS550 pulling up, she too dropped her mouth. "What the fuck! Carmelo letting you hold his whips now?" Tierra cracked, walking up on the driver's side where Nichelle was.

"Nope, this was a birthday present. Peep the tags."

Tierra strutted to the back of the car with an attitude in her switch. They damn sure were some vanity plates, with "NICHELLE" written on them. All she could do was shake her head before stepping in the passenger side.

Tierra was used to all eyes being on her because of her pretty face and small waist, but won't nobody on the block thinking about her at that moment. The only thing the males and females were lusting after was the official ride she was getting into.

"Yo, this shit is fire," Tierra admitted, not able to contain how fierce the whip was.

"I know, I couldn't believe when Carmelo surprised me with it. I had no idea he was gonna come at me so hard."

"And damn, Nichelle, I feel bad."

"Why?" she asked driving off.

"What type of best friend am I, that I didn't even

remember your birthday?"

"Don't worry about it. I know you've had a lot of shit on your mind."

"You have no idea. It's been hell being back home at my mom's crib. She be tryna regulate and preach to me at the same time. She be pressing me to enroll in community college…saying I need to learn a skill. I tried to explain to her that I do have a skill. It's just not the kind you can learn in a schoolbook," Tierra joked.

"You are ridiculous. But you never know you might enjoy taking some classes. I mean, I never thought I would love writing, but I do."

"So now you love writing?"

"Yep. I don't know if I'll ever be good enough to get published, or however it works, but when I'm doing it, I get this sense of peace that I don't get from anything else. That's why I say, maybe you should follow your mother's advice and enroll in school. What they always say… 'A mind is a terrible thing to waste'?" Both girls burst out laughing, and for the first time in awhile, it felt like old times again.

"So where we eating?"

"It's up to you."

"Girl, you know I want to check out our soul food spot up in the cut. I'm dying for some of that macaroni and cheese."

"Hell yeah, and some collard greens. That's exactly where we going," Nichelle said, making a left on Jamaica Avenue.

After a ten minute ride, the girls pulled up to

their favorite spot, ready to get their grub on. When they got to the door, walking up right behind them was a group of girls.

"If it ain't Nichelle Martin's stuck-up ass!" Tierra and Nichelle heard one of them snarl.

At first, Nichelle ignored whoever was popping shit behind her back, because she knew with any type of 'hood shine came hating. But the chick kept running her mouth.

"I bet she think she cute, 'cause she pushing some niggas' car. I wonder how much dick she had to swallow to make that happen." Her whole crew laughed extra hard, pumping her up.

"Ho, who the fuck you think you talking too?" Tierra turned around, walking up on the chicks.

"Tierra, don't even pay them birds no mind."

"Bitch, who you calling a bird?"

Nichelle looked up to see who wanted to bring it, and instantly recognized her enemy. "Lerrick, we ain't at school, and this isn't no playground. You and your crew can carry that drama somewhere else."

"You Lerrick Duncan, Kay Kay little sister?" Tierra asked, folding her arms.

"Yeah, why?"

"Because when we was in high school, I used to beat her ass on a regular 'cause she had a foul mouth just like you. And if you keep fuckin' around wit' my girl, Nichelle, I'ma spank yo' ass like I did your sister."

Lerrick and her crew went silent, sizing up both Tierra and Nichelle. There were four of them, but besides Lerrick, none of them was really the fighting type. They were all semi-looking chicks who thought they were certifiable dimes, and none of them were trying to exchange blows on Lerrick's account.

"You poppin' mad shit." Lerrick finally said something, not wanting to appear like she was backing down or afraid in front of her crew.

"That's because I'm always ready for whatever, but clearly you're not," Tierra spewed, turning to Nichelle with a smirk on her face.

Lerrick used that as an opportunity to sneak a hard shove on Tierra, which caused her to lose her balance and fall back against the entrance door to the restaurant. "I see you ain't got shit to say now!" Lerrick boasted.

"Tierra, you a'ight?" Nichelle ran over to help her friend up, but there was no need.

Tierra got up, charging like a raging bull. She clawed her nails into Lerrick's mug, gripping it so tightly you would've thought she was going to rip it off. "You wanna fuck wit' me? Is you fuckin' crazy? I'ma show you crazy, motherfucker! I got your crazy!" Tierra slammed Lerrick's body down to the concrete, and kept pounding her head back.

Lerrick's crew stood around in shock and amazement at how a seemingly non-threatening looking chick was putting a beat down on Lerrick like she was a straight up dude.

Tierra then clenched Lerrick's ponytail around her hand and gave her a closed-fist pounding, putting major damage on the right side of her face. As the blood began gushing out Lerrick's mouth, Nichelle became worried that Tierra was going to have her hospital-bound.

"Tierra, that's enough!" Nichelle screamed out, but Tierra wouldn't let up. "Come on, Tierra, that's enough!" Nichelle caught Tierra's fist midair, and held it as tight as she could.

Tierra jerked her body away and gave Lerrick one final slam on the ground. "Heffa, if you ever even *think* of breathing in my direction again, I will demolish yo' ass! You young ass heffas gon' learn to respect yo' elders…trick ass bitch!"

"Girl, let's go!" Nichelle rushed to her car, pulling Tierra's arm. She knew Tierra's temper, and once she got started, she would be ready to go all twelve rounds.

Lerrick was finally able to regain her composure, and watched in fury as Nichelle and Tierra drove away. She was in pain, angry and embarrassed all at the same time. "Yeah, g'on 'head and drive off. You got this first round, but them bitches is mine!" she promised.

When Radric and Renny pulled into the private driveway of the Murano high rise condominium by Center City, they at once noticed a Hershey honey, wearing a floor-length chinchilla fur coat and wide rimmed black sunglasses going into the building.

"Damn, that bitch is the business!" Radric commented, about to catch a hard-on.

"Yo, I think that's fuckin' Chanel. She must be here to see Arnez. Her and her sister some cold motherfuckers."

"Them the twins you was talking 'bout?"

"No doubt. Them some of the baddest bitches in Atlanta."

"What the fuck is you talking bout'? That bitch right there is one of the baddest in Atlanta, New York, Philly... fuck it, worldwide! Do she fuck wit' yo' cousin? 'Cause I need that in my life."

"Last I knew, he was hung up on this broad named Talisa. But shit, that don't mean nothing. He might be tappin' that. But focus, man. First money, then pussy."

"I got you. Let's do this."

The two men strolled into the 42-story glass edifice, with a curved façade and blue-tinted floor-to-ceiling windows, heading straight for the elevator. The chocolate-brown bombshell Radric was lusting over was nowhere in sight as they made their way to the top floor.

"If it isn't my favorite cousin," Arnez said, greeting Renny with a hug.

Radric could easily see the resemblance, as both were Cuban and black.

"Man, it's been too long. Ain't nothing like seeing family."

"Well, come in. I don't need you standing in the hallway."

"This is my partner, Radric I told you about."

"It's good to meet you."

"Likewise. Your crib is the business," Radric said, taking in all 2,400 square feet of pure luxury.

"Shit, I wouldn't expect nothin' less," Renny said, nudging Arnez. Renny didn't expect anything less from his older cousin. He knew what both were accustomed to. They had balled hard together over the many years, and played hard. Living a lavish lifestyle wasn't even an option, it was mandatory.

They were from the "Big Meech" generation, where their attitude was, if you want to live regular, then get a job. But they ain't out there hustling, taking penitentiary chances everyday to live regular. They was going to ball until they fallout, go to sleep and get up and start all over again.

"Can I get either one of you something to drink?"

"I'll take some water." Radric's mouth was dry from smoking blunts the entire ride.

"I'm good," Renny said, ready to handle his business and break out. He had a situation in New York to deal with, and only limited time for small talk.

"Chanel, bring me some bottle water," Arnez said, to her. Renny eyed Radric, acknowledging that the woman they saw must in fact be one half of the twin set.

"Let's have a seat outside," Arnez suggested, leading them to the balcony.

It was brick outside, and neither man wanted to be bothered with the cold air, but ever since Renny could remember, Arnez never liked to discuss business indoors. It could be the middle of a snowstorm, but if you wanted to chat about drugs and money, then you would have to brave the weather and confer with Arnez on his terms. He never trusted closed in confinements, because he felt it was too easy for the feds or police to hear and fully understand his conversation.

"Can I use your restroom?" Radric didn't like to use other people's bathrooms, but he could no longer hold his piss and wanted to release himself before drinking some water.

"No problem, there is one right there by the kitchen."

"Thanks." On his way to the bathroom, Radric was able to get a much better and closer look at the woman he had fallen in lust with. She was even sexier up-close, but something about her aura made him nervous. It was like she was created from steel, and he felt no woman should be that hard.

"Here you go." Chanel placed the bottle down on the table outside. "Long time no see, Renny."

"I know, but you still fine as ever. How is your sister holding up?"

"The best she can under the circumstances. I'm actually supposed to pay her a visit this weekend."

"I'm surprised that they didn't lock you up too. But that's good. At least with you out, she got somebody to handle the business and money on the outside. What's her legal representation looking like?'

"I'm working on that now. But you know, only the best for CoCo."

Renny nodded his head, thinking she needed to hurry the fuck up. Doesn't nobody want to be caged up like an animal, especially when you used to living a lavish lifestyle like CoCo.

"It was good seeing you, Renny."

"Yeah, likewise."

"I'll be inside, Arnez."

Renny watched as Chanel walked off, admiring every curve on her statuesque body.

"So, what's up wit' you and homegirl? I know it's been a minute, but last I remembered, you was going strong with that girl, Talisa."

"So much has changed in such a small amount of time."

"Is any of those reasons why you seem to be settling into Philly instead going back to Atlanta?"

"You can say that. I have some unresolved issues with Talisa and her new boyfriend, Genesis. I won't be leaving Philly until they're dealt with."

"It sounds personal."

"It is."

"If I'm not mistaken, one of your rules is, 'never personal, always business'."

"Rules are made to be broken, and this is one of those times."

"This nigga, Genesis must've really gotten under your skin, or do you just have it bad for Talisa?"

"A little of both. Let's leave it at that...your partner is coming."

"I hope ya'll ain't started discussing business without me," Radric smiled, grabbing the bottle water and taking a seat across from Arnez.

"Nope, we were waiting for you, and now that we're all here, let's get down to business." Arnez sat back and got comfortable. Negotiating new business prospects was one of his biggest thrills. New clients meant new money, which equaled a bigger payday if everything worked out as planned.

Although Arnez was making more money than he could probably ever spend, it didn't matter to him. Being in the game was like an addictive drug, but instead of trying to break the habit, he embraced it with open arms. With every new deal, that habit became stronger and more powerful. Arnez's addiction was now so bad, that the only way he could cure it was by death or jail. Since he knew the latter wasn't in the cards for him, he made each move with calculated caution. That same ruthless mentality carried over to his personal life too, and for that reason alone, he would be making Philly his new home until all the loose ends were neatly tied up.

Blur

When you turn your life over to the streets, you're taking a chance that you or someone you love may experience a tragedy so profound, that it will change the course of your life forever. Simple things you took for granted, you would now give anything to experience again. But time stops or turns back for no one, so all you're left to hold on to is memories of the past.

"Yo, Simone, you should'a been there. It was like the old school Tierra back in the day when she would go around the neighborhood looking for a fight," Nichelle said, giving a play by play of Tierra's fight with Lerrick.

"Man, that trick made me so mad when she did that sucker push. That fight was over a week ago, and I'm still hot over that shit!"

"Damn, I wish I could'a been there! I ain't seen you fight in a minute. Back in school, everybody knew not to fuck wit Tierra's ass. It was a known fact that if you couldn't beat a motherfucker wit' yo' fist, then you had a razor, a knife or somethin' to slice that ass up."

Tierra reached across the table and gave Simone

a high-five, knowing she was speaking nothing but the truth.

"Nichelle, you might need to start carrying yo' razor again, because trust me, that silly bitch gon' come at you on some payback shit."

"Fuck Lerrick! You the one that beat her ass," Nichelle giggled. "But seriously, if she know what's good for her, she'll stay the fuck away from me. I ain't neva stopped carrying my shit, and I have no problem using it."

"That's my girl! I raised you right," Tierra smiled at Nichelle.

"Sure the fuck did," Simone chimed in.

"So Simone, you hanging wit' me and Nichelle tonight? We going to Harlem Lanes."

"Harlem Lanes, bitch, I know you ain't bowling."

"Nah, some industry party is happening, and BET suppose to be filming some shit up in there. Hell, I'm tryna snatch me a baller. And if you know what's good, you need to roll so you can get you one too."

"Nichelle, I know you ain't looking for no baller. You already straight. Shit, I still can't believe Carmelo gave you that Benz for your birthday. That nigga must really love you," Simone reasoned.

Nichelle caught Tierra rolling her eyes about the comment. "Why you got to roll your eyes like that?"

"It' nothing."

"Say what's on your mind. You never hold your tongue no other time."

Tierra let out a deep sigh as if trying to hold back her thoughts before letting it out. "It just seems like Carmelo wants to keep you all to himself. He's jealous of any other friendships you have, especially the one you have wit' me. I was yo' dog before we even knew of a Carmelo, but he don't respect that. And I'll be honest, that shit bothers me."

"Yeah, he do be seeming a little salty. He didn't say a word to us when we sat down at that birthday party. I even smiled and spoke, but got nothing," Simone added.

"I understand what ya saying, but Carmelo's older than us, and he wants me to be more settled down."

"But you're only eighteen. You have to live your life too. All I'm saying is don't give up your identity over no man. My mother did that, and after my dad died, she ain't neva been the same."

"I hear you. But enough of this depressing talk. Simone, are you coming out wit' us?"

"Sorry ladies, I have to pass."

Both Nichelle and Tierra gave each other the 'what the fuck' look.

"What the hell is going on? You don't neva give up the opportunity to meet a baller." Tierra tapped her fingers on the table waiting for a response.

"I think I might've already met my baller, and we going out to dinner tonight."

"Is it the same nigga you told me you met at that birthday party?"

"Yep."

"You still kicking it wit' him?"

"I'm lost. What guy are you all talking about?" Nichelle asked, feeling left out of the conversation.

"She won't tell me. She's tryna keep that shit on the low."

"If everything goes smoothly tonight, then I'll give you a name tomorrow. Shit, I'm tryna be like you, Nichelle, and have a nigga wife me the fuck up."

"Good luck on that. I'll stick to having multiple sponsors, so I will be at Harlem Lanes tonight scheming my ass off."

"Let's go. I have to stop at home before we go out tonight."

"You have to be a good wifey and check in," Tierra teased.

"Whatever! I'ma drop your loud mouth off at home and I'll be back around seven to pick you up. Speaking of loud, Simone, where's my baby? I haven't heard nothing out of him. You know I love me some lil' Anthony."

"Oh, he wit' his daddy. I'ma need some private time wit' my boo after we go out to eat dinner."

"You better be careful. I know you and Ant aren't together no more, but that nigga might flip if he sees the next man in your crib. Especially after he moved all my furniture up in here."

"I knew this furniture looked familiar," Nichelle said, looking around Simone's apartment. "This same shit was in your crib. It look good though."

"It better look good, as much money as Lucci spent on it. And speaking of money, you late on your payment, Simone."

"I knew you was gon' bring that shit up. Stay right here." Simone got up from the table and went to her bedroom.

"I know she got an attitude, but I don't give a fuck. I gave her this furniture hella cheap, and I'm letting her make payments. Sh-i-i-it, she need to be grateful."

"I'm sure she is, Tierra."

"I can't tell by the way she was twisting her neck when she got up from the table."

"Be quiet, here she comes."

"Here's *all* your money!" Simone snapped, dropping a bunch of bills on the table in front of Tierra. Tierra swallowed hard before quickly scooping them up.

"Damn Simone, what you do, rob a bank?" Nichelle was playing, but she was curious as to where Simone got all the money from.

"My boo gave it to me. He said he didn't want his baby owing nobody nothing."

Tierra glanced up at Simone with the money securely in her hand. "Who the fuck is this boo you got? This shit ain't adding up. Nichelle gotta man, now Simone fuckin' wit' some nigga that's lacing her pockets. I'm the only one out here struggling...well not for long!"

"What that mean...not for long?"

"Nothing, Nichelle. Let's go. I know Simone needs to get ready for her 'boo' so we ain't gon' hold you up."

"Bye, bitches, I'll talk to ya' later. Don't forget, if all goes well, I'll let you know who my mystery man is. Smooches!"

"You so crazy. We'll talk to you later. Tell my

baby, Anthony, Auntie Nichelle said hello."

"I will."

"Aren't you curious who this man is in Simone's life?' Tierra asked Nichelle once they got in the car.

"Somewhat, but honestly, I'm glad she's happy and she got a man who is helping her out. I mean, her sorry baby daddy don't hardly do shit."

"Yeah, you right about that. He wouldn't even give her no money for my furniture."

"Tierra, that's not your furniture anymore, so let it go."

"You know what I mean. He told her that he and his boys moving it in her crib was payment enough. It's like don't you want your seed to have some nice shit… better yet, you know his trifling ass gon' be wanting to lay and sit on the shit."

"Exactly! That's why I hope this new cat she's fuckin' wit' treats her right. Simone deserves to be happy."

"Yeah, and so do I," Tierra mumbled under her breath.

When Nichelle got home, Carmelo was sitting in the living room, and she was reluctant to tell him she was going out with Tierra. She thought about the conversation she had earlier with Simone and Tierra, and felt she needed to be honest with him. They were her friends, and there was room in her life for all three of them.

"Hey baby, I missed you," Nichelle said, giving Carmelo a kiss.

"I missed you too. I wanted us to hang out tonight, maybe see a movie or go out to dinner, but I just found out I have to handle some business."
Nichelle thought this was a good time to tell Carmelo where she was going, since he already had plans.

"Well, then would you mind if I go out with Tierra tonight?" There was a lingering silence in the air that made Nichelle uncomfortable. "Carmelo, I know you don't like Tierra, but besides you, she is my best friend. I know you may never accept her, but don't ask me to shut her out my life."

"I wouldn't ask you to do that. I don't believe Tierra is worthy of your friendship, but if that's who you choose to have in your life, then so be it. I just ask that you don't have her in this crib, because I don't trust her."

"I can do that." Although Nichelle didn't think it was right that Tierra couldn't come over, since she lived there too, she decided not to get into a deep conversation about it. Things had been going so well between her and Carmelo, and the last thing she wanted was for a casual conversation to turn into an intense argument. She was willing to respect his wishes, for now, but hoped in the future he would realize that Tierra was a true friend to her, and he would embrace their friendship.

"Before I head out, I wanted to give you something."

"What? I hope it's not another gift. You've already

done too much for me."

"I could never do enough for you. You have such a huge heart, always willing to give everybody the benefit of the doubt. That's why I worry about you so much."

"As long as I have you to protect me, I'll be fine."

"For sure, but this is for you." Carmelo picked up an envelope that was on the table and handed it to Nichelle. She opened it and was confused.

"What is this?"

"It's the title to the Benz. It's paid in full, but I took it out of my name and put it in yours."

"Why? I don't need the car in my name. I know you got it for me."

"Because if anything happens to me, I want to make sure that you have it. When I picked out the color, rims, interior, everything about it was beautiful, unique and special, just like you."

"I love you so much, not because of the car or crib or all the things that you buy me, but because I know that you really love me as much as I love you." Nichelle held Carmelo tightly, as if she never wanted to let him go. She felt their bond was unbreakable, and each day it seemed to become stronger.

"Girl, I'm so glad we came. I see mad cute niggas up in here," Tierra said, sizing up every dude in the spot…and the women. She needed to get an idea what her competition was looking like.

"There is a full house. I never knew this spot was so nice. I've already counted over twenty plasma televisions, and every bowling lane got big leather couches for you to sit back and relax on. They even got a children's party room. Simone definitely has to come next time so we can bring lil' Anthony."

"Fuck all that, Nichelle. Let's go upstairs. That's where the sports bar is. You know crazy cute niggas at the bar."

Nichelle followed Tierra to the upstairs bar area. As soon as they stepped on the hardwood floor, some dude grabbed Tierra's arm, spitting game. Tierra gave him all of thirty seconds and moved on after seeing his jewelry and shoe game wasn't to her liking.

The ladies then found two stools at the bar and sat down. They both sat in silence for a few minutes as Tierra examined all her potential prospects. Nichelle knew what she was doing, so she purposely sat in silence not to interrupt her mission.

Right when Tierra felt the upstairs action was a bust, a cutie approached her that had excellent probability written all over him. "What's your name, sexy?" the tall, Chris Brown look-alike asked. Light skinned men weren't really Tierra's taste, but he had a little ruggedness thing going on that she could work with.

"Tierra, and this is my friend Nichelle. What's your name?"

Nichelle simply nodded her head to say what's up. She never got too friendly with Tierra's potential prospects, because there was no telling how long she would keep them around.

"Theron. So, can I get you ladies something to drink?"

"No, we straight."

"Well, how about we go to the VIP lounge and talk? There isn't a place for me to sit at the bar, and I want a chance to talk to you... get to know you a little better."

"That sounds like a plan to me. Come on Nichelle, Theron is going to take us to the VIP lounge."

Nichelle grabbed her purse and followed behind them. When they got there, that's where BET was filming some segment. The mood was much more upbeat and there were a lot of scantily dressed women, even though it was dead in the middle of winter.

"I'm sitting over here." Theron directed them to the rust orange couch against the brick wall. There were a few other guys sitting there and a couple of women. Tierra glanced at the other dudes to see if she found any of them more appealing than Theron, but from first look, it seemed he was the catch of the crop.

Nichelle sat patiently as Tierra and Theron chatted it up. Tierra decided to have a glass of champagne, but Nichelle declined. At this point, she was bored and thought any sort of liquor would put her to sleep. She kept eyeing her watch, hoping that Tierra would be ready to leave soon. A few men would come over to try and kick it with Nichelle, but she would give them all the blank face stare, so they got the hint and kept it moving, except for one.

"Can I speak to you for a minute?" At first Nichelle

simply ignored him like she did with the two previous guys, but dude wasn't going for that. "Hello, can I have a word with you?"

This time Nichelle looked up and gave him the blank face stare. That look normally always worked to get rid of a man. But the dude persisted. "What do you want?"

"Aren't *you* friendly," he countered sarcastically.

"Listen, I have a man, and I'm not interested in talking to you, so can you go bother somebody else."

"Actually, I wanted to speak to you about business."

"Business? Dude, I'm in high school. There can be no business you can discuss with me."

"Wow, you're young! Are you at least eighteen?"

"Yeah, but what does that have to do with anything?" Nichelle was quickly getting annoyed and wanted the man to go away."

"My name is Akil, and I saw you and your friend when you first walked in."

"Hum hum…" Nichelle was letting it be known he was irritating her, and he needed to hurry up and get to the point.

"I'm working on something in the next few months, and I need a model."

"Again, what does that have to do with me?"

"I think you would be perfect."

"As the model?"

Akil smiled, and Nichelle stared at him and didn't know whether to laugh or tell him he needed to step it up and come with better game when trying to get a girl in bed. Instead, she kept it simple, because she didn't feel like having any drama. "No thanks."

"You must think I'm joking, but I'm serious."

"No thank you, I'm not interested," she said firmly, hoping that this time he would know she meant business.

"What's your name?"

"Nichelle, why?"

"Nichelle, take my business card. If you change your mind, give me a call. I'll definitely remember you."

"I'm sure you will," Nichelle smacked, as he walked away. "Tierra, are you ready to go yet? Because I need to get home."

"Yeah, I was about to tell you let's bounce. Theron, it was good meeting you, but me and my girl about to roll out."

"I'll call you tomorrow. Maybe we can go out to dinner."

"That might work. I'll let you know," Tierra said, not wanting to appear too anxious. Tierra reciprocated Theron's slight hug and headed out. "Girl, he's a cutie, and I think he got some chips. I might have to try him out."

"You do that."

"And I saw you talking to a cutie yourself? Who was he?"

"A nobody trying to sell me some modeling dream, thinking I would give him some ass." Nichelle looked down at the business card he gave her before tossing it in the trashcan.

117

"I wonder how Simone's date with her boo went tonight," Nichelle thought out loud as she drove over the Queensboro Bridge.

"I know, right? I have an idea."

"What?"

"Let's drive past her crib. She said after dinner they was going back to her place."

"What is driving past her crib gonna do? What, you gon' knock on the front door?"

"No! But, we might recognize the nigga's car parked out front, and we won't need for her to tell us who her so called boo is 'cause we'll already know."

"Girl, you might be reaching. Ain't no telling who she fucking wit'."

"Just drive past her crib, it can't hurt. It ain't like we going out our way. We have to go in that direction to get to my place."

"Fine. You so damn nosey."

"Stop acting like you don't want to know too."

"You right, I am curious, especially after that money she gave you. Whoever dude is, he can't be hurting too bad in the money department."

"Exactly. And let's be clear, ain't many niggas hitting bitches off wit' paper right now. The recession done worked its way all the way up to Wall Street and down to 'Hood Street."

"Tierra, you ain't got no damn sense!" Both ladies laughed as Nichelle turned onto Simone's block.

"Slow down," Tierra said. "I need to look at each car carefully to see if I recognize one. Oh, no the fuck!"

"What?" Nichelle put her foot on the brake,

nervous by Tierra's outburst.

"Nichelle, go up a little bit more. I think that's that sorry ass Radric's Range Rover up there. I know Simone wouldn't be fuckin' wit' Radric's ass behind my back...and that nigga giving her money! I got something for both of their asses!"

"Tierra, calm the fuck down! You might be jumping to conclusions. We don't even know if that's Radric's car."

"We 'bout to find the fuck out!" Tierra jumped out the Benz and ran up to the truck. There was another Range Rover parked right beside it.

The very next second they both heard sirens, and Nichelle looked in her rearview mirror, noticing the police cars were coming in their direction.

"What the hell is going on?" Nichelle rolled down her window and stuck her head out, "Tierra, get back in the car." But Tierra stood there frozen, not making a move.

"Put your hands up!" the police officer yelled, pointing a gun towards Tierra's back.

Nichelle saw a couple of people looking out of their windows, and a few came and stood on top of their front stairs. She was waiting for Simone to come out and clown them for lurking on her block. She waited for a few minutes to see what the police officers were going to say to Tierra, but when she saw them putting her in handcuffs, Nichelle knew she had to see what was going on.

"Excuse me officer, but why are you putting handcuffs on my friend?"

"This woman is with you?"

"Yes, we just got here. We came to see a friend of ours who lives right there," Nichelle explained, pointing to the building Simone lived in.

"We haven't been able to get two words out of her. Maybe she's in shock."

"Shock over what?"

"This is a crime scene. I'm going to need for you to move back," the officer ordered Nichelle.

She walked over to Tierra, who was sitting in the backseat of the police car with the door open.

"Is she under arrest?" Nichelle asked the other officer, totally puzzled by what was going on.

"Not yet," he answered coldly.

"Then can you take these handcuffs off of her?"

Without warning, Tierra bent over and vomited on the ground, getting some on Nichelle's boots. "Tierra, are you alright? Would you please help my friend!" Nichelle screamed out.

By this time, more police officers were on the scene, and the ambulance had showed up.

While one of the officers tended to Tierra, and with all the chaos going on, Nichelle used the opportunity to see what had her best friend so shaken. She quickly ran up to the two Range Rovers that were parked side by side, and when she got a clear view of the crime scene, everything became a blur, then she fainted, knocking herself unconscious as her head hit the concrete.

Welcome To Heartbreak

Do you really believe it's better to have found love and lost it, than to never have found love at all? I suppose that's a question that only each individual knows the answer to. But street love is some of the strongest around. It's the kind that never dies.

"No, no, this isn't happening! Somebody help me, pleeeeease!" Nichelle screamed out, fighting her way through a nightmare.

"It's okay, baby, I'm right here," Nichelle's mother whispered, holding her daughter as she awoke from her sleep.

Nichelle was breathing hard and drenched in sweat. "Where am I?" she asked, opening her eyes. When she tried to sit up, she let out a sigh. "My head is killing me," she said, feeling the knot on the back of her head. She turned and saw Tierra standing behind her mother, who was still holding her.

"You're in the hospital. Tierra, can you go let the doctor know that Nichelle woke up?"

"Sure, Ms. Martin, I'll be right back."

"Ma, what's going on? Why am I in the hospital?"

"You don't remember what happened last night?"

Nichelle closed her eyes, and images of what she saw started flashing in her head. She tried shaking them out of her mind, because she didn't want to believe they were real.

"No...no...no! Ma, this can't be real! Simone can't be dead!" she cried with tears flooding down her face. "And Carmelo...Oh God, Carmelo is dead too!" she covered her face with her hands and just wept uncontrollably.

When Tierra came back in with the doctor and saw Nichelle crying, she ran over and hugged her. "I'm so sorry, Nichelle. I can't believe Carmelo, Radric and Simone are all dead."

"Oh my goodness, Tierra, Radric was in the truck! He was in the truck with Carmelo!" It was all beginning to come back to Nichelle. "Simone was in the other Range Rover, but who was she with?'

"That dude, Marley."

The name sounded familiar to Nichelle, but she couldn't remember where she heard it from.

Tierra could tell Nichelle was having a hard time, so she tried to jog her memory. "Remember the dude's birthday party we went to awhile back?"

"That's right, he was Carmelo's people. I remember him saying they did business together."

"Ladies, I know you're going through a hard time and I don't want to interrupt, but Nichelle, I need to examine you quickly and make sure you're okay," the doctor said.

"Sure," Nichelle said, in a daze. While the doctor

examined Nichelle, Tierra sat down in the chair next to Ms. Martin.

"That could've been you and Nichelle in one of those cars shot dead," Ms. Martin said, solemnly. "I don't know when you girls gon' learn that these streets don't love nobody. If these tragic and senseless murders don't make you girls stay away from street thugs, I don't know what will.

Tierra understood that Ms. Martin meant well, but she wasn't trying to hear it. Her daddy was a hustler of the streets, every man she ever dealt with was a hustler on the streets, and she too hustled the streets. To dismiss all of that would be like dismissing herself and the people she loved and respected. Risking your life was one of the downsides of being in the game, but the upsides were so much more—fast money, designer clothes, bad ass cribs and cars. You could never get that breaking your back everyday working a nine to five.

Tierra was devastated by the deaths of Radric, Simone, and even Carmelo, but when you play the game, you know that you can also die from the game.

The next day, Nichelle left the hospital and went to stay at her mother's place. She wasn't ready to go back to the home she shared with Carmelo. Part of her still hadn't accepted that he was dead. She kept replaying the last kiss they shared, the last words he spoke, and how it felt the last time he wrapped his arms around her.

"Nichelle, are you sure you don't want me to spend the night with you? Your mother's at work, and I hate for you to be alone."

"I appreciate the offer, Tierra, but I'll be fine. I'm not gonna be doing nothing but staying in bed and cry all night anyway."

"That's okay, I can stay and cry with you."

"I guess God knew what he was doing by keeping you around, because I don't know what I would do if he took you away from me too." Nichelle's eyes filled with tears as the loneliness of losing the love of her life engulfed her.

"You don't have to worry, God don't want no part of me. I'm much too scandalous for what He got going on up there," Tierra said, pointing her finger up. "He gon' keep me right here on Earth so I can continue to create havoc for the rest of the crazy people like me. Plus, He knows I have to protect you. You're one of the good ones."

"I always thought Carmelo would be here to protect me. It's like I can't breathe." Nichelle held her pillow tightly to her chest and soaked it with tears.

Tierra wanted to console her friend, but there wasn't anything she could do. She knew Nichelle would have to deal with the pain of losing Carmelo in her own way, and in her own time. All she could do was be there for her through the process. "Would you like for me to get you anything before I leave, Nichelle?"

"No," she said, choking back her tears. "Have you had a chance to talk to Simone's mother?"

"Yeah. Of course she's taking it hard. Then poor lil' Anthony, he's only a baby, but he can tell something ain't right. When I was there, he was looking around as if he was waiting for his mother to walk through the door. That shit tore me up."

"I know. My heart breaks for that little boy, having to grow up without his mother."

"And then that piece of shit daddy he got. Do you know that nigga was talking shit about Simone in front of lil' Anthony and her mother?"

"Saying what?"

"That if Simone hadn't been fucking wit' a known drug dealer like Marley, she wouldn't of been shot dead."

"That nigga got some nerve!"

"Yeah, especially since he do the same dirt. He a jealous nigga, because Marley was a major player in the game, and he was and will always be a low level pusher. That shit ate him up that Simone had upgraded to a real boss."

"I guess we finally found out who her mystery boo was. Too bad it had to be under these circumstances," Nichelle said, tossing her pillow on the floor. "The cops still don't have any idea who's responsible?"

"No, and with all the unsolved murders in New York, I doubt they ever will or care to."

"How did the cops even know to come there?"

"From what I was told, somebody that lived on Simone's block heard gunshots and called the police. But of course, nobody saw nothing or actually witnessed the murders."

"Do you think it was a robbery? And why was Carmelo in the car with Radric?" Nichelle wondered.

"Maybe they were doing business together. I don't know."

"I have so many questions and not enough answers. Four people shot dead, and don't nobody know shit. Welcome to Queens!"

The day of Carmelo's funeral finally arrived, and Nichelle dreaded going. She still hadn't gone back to their condo, but felt it was time to do so. But first, she needed to go and watch Carmelo be put to rest. That was going to take all her strength, and she was relieved that Tierra was going with her. She wanted her mother to escort her too, but like always, she had to work.

"Tierra, I know Carmelo wasn't a friend of yours, in fact you didn't even like him, so thank you so much for going with me. I could never handle this by myself."

"And you shouldn't have to. Yeah, Carmelo and I weren't friends, but you and I are. I want to be here for you." Tierra gently grabbed Nichelle's hand and held it until they got out of the car to go inside the church where the funeral was being held.

When they entered the church, it was jammed packed. Nichelle recognized a few familiar faces from around the way, but mostly everyone else seemed to be strangers. Carmelo had kept Nichelle so isolated from his business and never talked much about his family, that it wasn't until this moment Nichelle realized how much she didn't know about his life. Tierra found a seat for them near the back of the church, as the service had already started, and they didn't want to attract attention to themselves.

After the reverend finished giving a beautiful sermon, a young girl, who looked to be no more than eleven, stood up and sang a song. Midway through, the little girl broke down and cried and ran to a woman wearing a black sable fur coat.

"I hate funerals," Tierra grumbled, trying not to tear up over how distraught the young girl seemed to be.

The reverend then stood back up and said a few more words before everybody stood up to go pay their last respects.

"At least Carmelo was able to have an open casket," Nichelle said as she stood up to go view his body. "Will you walk with me?" She looked over at Tierra who was still sitting down.

"Of course."

When Nichelle got to the casket, she paused for a moment prior to going forward. She wanted to gain her composure before seeing Carmelo's dead body. When she stood over him, he looked so peaceful, as if he was sleeping. She kissed her two fingers and placed them on top of Carmelo's lips. "I'll never stop loving you, baby. My heart will always belong to you." A single tear rolled down her face. She headed towards the exit door, knowing that was the last time she would ever see or touch the man she loved more than anything in this world again.

"Tierra, wait up," they heard someone call out as they were walking to Nichelle's car. They both turned around to see who it was.

"Renny, hey, I'm surprised to see you here."

"Yeah, I wanted to pay my respects."

"You knew Carmelo?" Nichelle asked softly.

"I had met him recently through Marley. We were all doing some business together."

"I guess that means you knew Radric too."

"Yes, he was one of my closest friends."

"I'm so sorry for you loss."

"I'm sorry for yours too. You were Carmelo's girlfriend, right? I think I saw you a couple of times with him."

"Yes."

"I know how difficult it must be to lose a loved one. I'll keep you in my prayers."

"Thank you, I truly appreciate that," Nichelle muttered, not wanting to shed more tears.

"Tierra," Renny said, turning his attention to her. "I was surprised I didn't see you at Radric's funeral yesterday."

"I don't like funerals. The only reason I came to this one was to support Nichelle."

"I'm sure you'll be going to Simone's though, right?"

"Of course, she was a very close friend of mine."

"I'm not going to hold you ladies up anymore, but Nichelle," Renny reached out and took her hand. "Please take care of yourself."

"I'll try."

"Come on, Nichelle, we need to go." Tierra pulled Nichelle's arm away, thinking Renny was holding on to her hand way too long.

Renny stood and watched Tierra and Nichelle get in the car. He could tell how vulnerable Nichelle was, and that this would be the time to make his move. But, he also reasoned that he would have to be very careful with his approach. She was a young lady in a great deal of pain, so being too aggressive would push her away. He wasn't worried though. He was a master at manipulation, and he would figure out a way to win Nichelle over.

Nichelle stood with the key in the lock for a minute before opening the door. Part of her felt like she was doing too much in one day. First the funeral, now walking into the home she shared with Carmelo. *I can do this*, she thought to herself and opened the door.

When she set foot in the entrance, she was flooded with memories. She thought about how Carmelo let her pick out all the furniture and decorate the place how she wanted. She looked over at the glass fireplace, and thought about the numerous times they made love in front of it.

Instead of being sad, Nichelle actually felt a sense of happiness being back in the place where they shared so many wonderful memories. She walked over to her favorite picture of the two of them. It was from their trip to the Bahamas. It was the very first time

Nichelle had ever been out of the State of New York. Until that day, she didn't even know water that blue or sand so white existed. Staring at that photo, for the first time since his death, Nichelle was able to smile. But then, just as quickly thinking about his death turned her smile into a frown.

"I hated saying goodbye to Carmelo, but I'm glad that funeral is over with. Being in that church with all those strangers and unable to grieve the way I wanted to, made me feel like I was about to suffocate."

"I know what you mean. I'm dreading going to Simone's funeral. It's depressing. I want to remember all the good times we shared together, not that she's gone. I don't believe Simone would want us mourning for her. If anything, she would want us to party."

"Yeah, Simone always loved a good party."

"How do you feel being back here?" Tierra asked, quickly changing the subject, not wanting to dwell on how hard she was taking Simone's death.

"A lot better than I thought I would. Nothing is going to bring Carmelo back, but being here lets me feel his presence, if that makes any sense."

"I'm not the sentimental type, but it actually makes a lot of sense. Does that mean you're going to continue to live here even though he's gone?"

"Wow that is something to think about. I know I can't afford to pay any of the bills. Hell, even if I could, I wouldn't know how or who to pay the bills to."

"Maybe you should take whatever you want to keep, and then sell the rest. Put the money you make away and move back in with your mom until you decide what you wanna do. It's a suggestion. I mean it would be hard for anybody to walk away from a crib this fly, but the cost to maintain it has to be ridiculously high. You don't need that type of stress."

"You're right about that."

"You don't have to make any decisions right away, but at least you have an option."

Knock...knock...knock

"Who could that be?" Nichelle wondered out loud when she heard the knocking at the front door.

"The only way you gon' find out is to open the door, because I definitely don't have a clue."

Nichelle looked through the peephole, but whoever was out there wasn't standing within her view. "Who is it?" she asked.

"Carmelo's people," a man replied.

Nichelle reluctantly opened the door, yet interested to see who his so-called people were. Tierra walked up behind Nichelle, carrying her purse. There was a knife inside, and Tierra was ready to use it if anything jumped off.

When Nichelle opened the door, there was a man and woman standing next to each other.

"How can I help you?"

"You're Nichelle, correct?" the woman asked with anger in her voice.

"Yes, and who are you?"

"I'm Carmelo's wife, and this is my brother."

Nichelle's heart dropped, and she tipped back as if about to fall, but Tierra held her up so she wouldn't lose her balance.

After Nichelle regained her composure, Tierra stepped forward, wanting to be seen. She didn't want the man and woman to think Nichelle was alone and they could bum rush her. "You must be mistaken, because Carmelo wasn't married. He's my boyfriend—I mean *was* my boyfriend—before he got killed."

"No, sweetie, you were his *mistress,* because I'm his wife!" she said, flinging her hand with the wedding ring on it. Nichelle covered her mouth, trying to stop the quivering of her lips.

"I don't give a damn if you was or wasn't Carmelo's wife, because he ain't wit' us no more anyway. So what in the hell do you want?" Tierra yelled, not giving a damn who she was, but pissed that she was upsetting Nichelle so much.

While Tierra and the woman bickered back and forth, Nichelle stared at her intently. She remembered the woman from the funeral. She was still wearing the black sable fur coat. "Was that Carmelo's daughter who was singing at the funeral?"

Everybody went silent, and all eyes were on Nichelle. Tierra could see the tears building up in Nichelle's eyes, and her heart broke for her.

"Yes, it was. We have two kids together; a son and a daughter."

"I had no idea," Nichelle disclosed, turning her head away.

"Yeah, but obviously married or not, you knew about Nichelle, because you came looking for her. She damn sure wasn't looking for you!" Tierra spit.

"Listen—"

"No, you listen!" Tierra jumped in, cutting her off. "Clearly you wanted Nichelle to know you were married to Carmelo, so mission accomplished. Now, you can leave."

"I ain't done accomplishing all my shit. I want you out my crib," the woman turned to Nichelle and said.

"Excuse me! This is the home I shared with Carmelo. It isn't your crib."

"When are you young, silly girls gon' learn. Whose name do you think this place was in? He was a drug dealer, for heavens sake! You think he can put an expensive ass condo in his name? No, this shit is in *my* name. Look at the papers." The woman practically shoved them down Nichelle's throat. "It says 'Lynette Clayton', that's me. So I need you to get your shit and get out!"

"She ain't leaving tonight. She needs time to get her stuff together. I mean this has been her home with *your* husband for how many months now? You wanna throw around words like 'young' and 'silly', but who's really the clown in this situation? You know that your husband is laying up with a teenager every fuckin' night, taking care of her while you stuck at home taking care of his kids. This crib might be in your name, but the same shit he was buying you, trust, he was lacing her wit' too.

And see, I had a daddy that was married to my mother, but unlike you he lived in the house wit' us. He was also a drug dealer, hustling dope making serious paper. But when he got killed, my mother couldn't afford to maintain that lifestyle that he had given us, so we ended up back in the projects. And I guarantee you, so will you and your kids. So don't come around here actin' like you better than somebody 'cause you got a ring on your finger."

"That's enough!" her brother barked, seeing that his sister was visibly shaking with the lashing Tierra was giving her.

"You have forty-eight hours to get out my home, or next time, I'll bring the police and they'll put you out."

"Mrs. Clayton, you must not be from New York. If you were, you would know the housing laws. See, Nichelle gets mail here and has been a resident for over thirty days. You can't just throw her out of shit. There's a legal procedure you have to go through... you feel me?"

You could see the fire steaming from the woman's head, and it made Tierra's smile get wider and wider.

"I'll be out by tomorrow."

"Nichelle, fuck this bitch! You don't have to rush and leave."

"I want to leave. Now excuse me, I need for you to go...now!" Nichelle didn't wait for a response, she just slammed the door in Lynette and her brother's face.

"You better than me. I would stay up in this motherfucker until I was dragged out just to spite that bitch."

"It ain't even worth it. He was married and had kids with another woman. I mean, did I even know this man?" Nichelle sat down on the couch, shaking her head out of frustration and heartache.

"You know that he loved you."

"Did he really? Can someone really love you and deceive you like that?"

"You know I was neva a fan of Carmelo's, but I will say this. That nigga loved you. And don't you let his bitter wife or anybody else convince you otherwise. I have been around the block a few times, and ain't no nigga ever treated me half as good as Carmelo treated you. He wasn't doing it either, because you were some trick. He did it out of love."

"But why didn't he tell me he was married with kids?"

"You ain't gon' ever understand why men do some of the shit they do. And trust, I'm not condoning what Carmelo did, but a nigga has always, and will always continue to do fucked up shit and break a woman's heart. That's why I ain't got one. But, baby girl, you one of the lucky ones. You found real love. It may have ended up being somewhat tainted, but it don't change the fact that the shit was real."

"In my heart I feel the same way, but finding out about his wife and kids makes some things confusing."

"What things?"

"When I was at the hospital, the doctor told me I was eight weeks pregnant. I had no idea. But when I first found out, I wanted to keep our baby."

"What about now?"

"I still do. I can't imagine killing the child growing inside of me. It's Carmelo's baby. I would be able to forever have a part of him, even though he's no longer with me."

"Nichelle, the thought of that is beautiful, but with a baby comes a lot of responsibility. You haven't even graduated from high school yet. Then you have to find a way to financially take care of the baby. Do you really want your son or daughter to grow up in the projects like we did?"

"I'll find a way to make it work. This baby is my attachment to Carmelo. I won't let that go...I can't."

See Me In Your Nightmares

There is no escaping karma when you do dirt. Payback will surly find you. Unfortunately, you never know when, where or from whom that retaliation will come from. At the very moment you believe you have escaped from having to answer for the misfortune you've caused another, that is when you meet your demise.

Nichelle took one last look at the place she had called home for what now seemed like a lifetime. She had left everything, from the furniture to the paintings on the walls. The only thing she was leaving with was her personal belongings and a few pictures of her and Carmelo.

"Girl, you crazy for leaving all this shit instead of selling it. You know that bitter ass Lynette gon' turn around and do exactly that, then pocket all the money. I wouldn't let that bitch get shit, especially for how she came at you on some real disrespectful shit."

"She can have it. They are only material things. The stuff that really matters, I'm taking with me."

"You need to stop with all that being saintly shit.

You got a child to think about now, and how you gon' feed him or her."

"Tierra, I'm far from a saint, and I'm not tryna' be one. All I want to do is move on with my life. Selling shit and battling with Carmelo's wife isn't gonna bring him back or make my situation any less painful."

"Whatever!" Tierra rolled her eyes. "But when that belly start poking out and reality kick in, don't say I didn't tell you that you should've unloaded this shit like you a booster."

What Tierra was saying did make a lot of sense to Nichelle. She would need money to take care of her child, and a lot of it. But what Tierra didn't understand was that Nichelle was too emotionally drained and depressed to go to combat with anyone. The only reason she forced herself to get out of bed, eat and take minimal care of herself was because she knew that the seed growing inside her needed that to survive.

"Come on, let's go. I'm done here." Before Nichelle walked out, she glanced around the condo before placing her key on the kitchen counter. But this time, there would be no tearful goodbye or regrets. She was closing the door on that part of her life she shared with Carmelo, and focusing on the future life that they created.

Lynette was on her third shot of Patron, impatiently waiting for the person she was supposed to be meeting. She eyed her watch, becoming heated, realizing he was more than an hour late. "Fuck that!" she hissed, slamming the glass down after gulping down her fourth shot. "This nigga ain't showing up. I can't believe he wasted my time." She left some money to cover her bill and decided to break out.

"Leaving so soon?"

"I've been waiting here for over an hour! What the fuck took you so long?"

"Have a seat and calm down. You're embarrassing yourself and me."

Lynette did what he said, mainly because the effect of the alcohol was taking its toll on her. If she didn't sit down, there was a very good chance she would fall and bust her ass. "I'm calm. Now, did you bring me my money?" Lynette cut to the chase, because it was all about the dollar for her.

"I got it, but I need details first."

"What you wanna know?"

"For one, how did Nichelle take the news?"

"How the fuck you think she gon' take it? A woman shows up at your door telling you that the man you were playing house with and in love with is actually married. I don't give a fuck who you are, that news ain't gon' sit well with nobody."

"Did you tell her to get out of his crib because the shit is in your name?"

"Of course! That shit is true, even though I ain't thinking about that condo or who's living in it."

"I know you didn't say that shit?"

"Of course not. I kept to the script, although I was ready to take off my boot and beat her friend's ass.

That bitch had the nerve to try and school me on my marriage."

"You must be talking about Tierra," he smiled, imagining Tierra cutting up. "Did Nichelle agree to leave?"

"Yep, she said she would be out today. I don't know how true that is and I really don't care. I'm ready to take my ass back to Houston, and as soon as you give me my money, that's what I'm gonna do."

"Entertain my curiosity for one second, then I'll give you your money and you're free to go."

"What is it?"

"It doesn't bother you the slightest that your husband was in a serious relationship with another woman and living with her?"

"Listen, my marriage with Carmelo had *been* over. I wasn't a bit more married to him than I am to that stranger sitting over there in that corner. By the time he got serious with that girl, we were married in name only. Our relationship was nothing more than a convenient business arrangement at that point. But neither of us felt the need to get a divorce, because I wasn't stopping him from doing what he wanted to do, and he wasn't stopping me from doing the same."

"But what about your kids?"

"He always took excellent care of our kids and would visit with them on a regular. I had no complaints. Now with him dead, shit done changed. I ain't never worked. I always depended on Carmelo to take care of us. But I refuse to be like the rest of these women, and me and my kids end up in the projects struggling because I decided to marry the game, but it divorced me before my time was up. That's why when you offered to hit me off with a bunch of money, and all I had to do was crush the dreams of some bright-eyed, dumbass teenager, I jumped at it."

"It's good to know you won't be losing any sleep over it."

"Hell no! She's young. Her fast ass will find some other rich thug and forget all about Carmelo."

"I hope you're right." The man pulled out the money from his coat pocket and handed it to Lynette.

"Thank you. I'm gon' put this money to good use." Lynette then flipped through the hundred dollar bills, making sure every dollar he promised was there, not even feeling the need to be discreet.

"I'm sure you will."

"Do you mind entertaining *my* curiosity for a second before I roll outta here?" Lynette asked, feeling extra confident now that her pockets were swollen.

"Ain't nothing wrong with even exchange."

"Cool. So tell me the real reason you contacted me after Carmelo got killed."

"I told you. Carmelo and I were doing business together, and when I heard he had a wife and kids, I figured you might need some help."

"Okay, I'll accept that. But what about you making it a condition that the only way I would get the money was if I let that girl know I was his wife?"

"She had the right to know. You know how you said she would find another thug and forget about Carmelo...well by you telling her that he was never hers to begin with, will make it much easier for her to do just that."

"You mean easier for her to move on to you." Lynette smacked her lips, letting Renny know she was hip to his game.

"Not necessarily me, but whomever she decides to kick it with."

"Yeah, right! You know you're itching for some of that young tight pussy. But, I advise you to be careful. Manipulating your way into somebody's heart is the quickest way to get yours broken."

"Oh, you're a comic now. With that money I gave you, you can take your show on the road."

"Joke if you like, but I'm an old school ho that has been around the block many times...too many to count. When you're young like that little girl, Nichelle, you're resilient. By the time you get my age, you're too fuckin' tired to care. Your only concern is that all your financial needs be met, and to be left alone. But men like you ain't satisfied until they have it all, and there is where the problem lies." Lynette stood up, happy she was no longer feeling light on her feet. "Nice doing business with you, Renny, and good luck—you're gonna need it."

Lynette slid her fingers though her short-cropped hair, feeling good about her brief visit. She got what she needed from Renny, and couldn't wait to get the hell out of New York. Her job there was done. She buried her husband, and at the same time, was able to finance her future, which meant using her new money to lure in a new baller.

Nichelle sat in class, depressed, tired, and nauseous. She already missed a week of school dealing with the loss of Carmelo, and couldn't afford to get any further behind in her work. With a baby on the way, she was determined to graduate. At the very least, she needed a high school diploma if she wanted a chance to give her child any sort of future.

"Mr. Chambers, can I speak with you for a minute?" Nichelle asked after the bell rang and class was over.

"Sure. I wanted to talk with you anyway. I heard some students in one of my earlier classes discussing what happened to a friend of yours, and your boyfriend. I'm sorry. I know that must be very difficult."

"It is, but I'm trying to hold it together. That's why I haven't been in school. I know I've never been a model student," Nichelle nervously giggled, "but I really want to do better. That's why I wanted to talk to you about working on my writing. I want to get serious about it, even maybe one day have a career doing it."

"Are you serious?" he questioned, sounding pleasantly surprised.

"Yes. With the loss of my boyfriend, it helped me put a lot of things into perspective. I want to concentrate on getting myself together and turn my life around."

"I'm proud of you, Nichelle, and I'll do whatever I can to help you accomplish that."

"Thank you. I needed to hear that. Where I'm from, I don't have dream-believers, I'm surrounded with dream-killers."

"Not with me. Everything starts with a dream, and if I have my way, all of yours will come true."

"Mr. Chambers, can you excuse me for one second? I'll be right back."

"Nichelle, are you okay?" he questioned, seeing the grimaced expression on her face.

"I need to go to the bathroom. It must have been something I ate at lunch. It ain't sitting well on my stomach. I'll be back though, so we can talk some more…if that's okay?"

"Of course. I'll be here for a while, going through papers. Comeback when you're done."

"Thanks." Nichelle couldn't get out the classroom fast enough. Her nausea was on overdrive, and thought if she stayed any longer, she was going to puke all over her teacher. By the time she reached the bathroom, she barely made it to the stall, vomiting half in the toilet and half on the floor.

"Damn, this pregnancy shit is no joke!" Right when Nichelle reached over to get some toilet tissue to wipe her mouth, round two kicked in, and her head was back over the toilet, vomiting some more.

In between barfing, she could hear voices and people coming in an out the restroom, but she didn't think anything of it, until the bathroom door that she didn't have time to lock came flinging open and knocked her down on the floor. The side of her face and clothes were saturated with her vomit. Before she even had a chance to look up and react, somebody clawed their hands in the crown of her head, dragging her out the stall.

"Look what we got here! You look like shit, and you stink, with all the vomit on you," Lerrick teased, standing in front of Nichelle while two of her crew held her. "I see you ain't got your pitbull in a skirt, so now what you gon' do?" Lerrick mocked.

"Lerrick, I don't want no beef, and I don't want to fight you," Nichelle coughed, still feeling the need to throw up again.

"Oh, poor thang! You in mourning 'cause yo' nigga dead! That's what yo' uppity ass get! I guess it's back to the 'hood for you!" Lerrick and her crew laughed, getting a kick out of Nichelle's current predicament. "Well, fuck you!" Lerrick said, spitting in Nichelle's face.

As the spit rolled down the bridge of Nichelle's nose, her insides were boiling up in anger. But she tried to remain calm, thinking about the safety of the baby she so desperately wanted growing inside of her. "Lerrick, you and your girls have had your fun. You spit on me and got me looking stupid. Now, can you please just let me go? No hard feelings." Tears began welling up in Nichelle's eyes because she knew how vulnerable she was at that very moment.

"Ahhh, are you scared, Nichelle?" Lerrick continued her cruel taunts.

"No, I'm pregnant, and I'm thinking about my baby right now, so please do the right thing and let me go."

"Bitch, please! I ain't letting nothin' go!" With that, Lerrick began her punishment on Nichelle, first landing a couple of blows to her face. "I see you ain't got no slick shit to say now," Lerrick goaded, knowing Nichelle was defenseless to retaliate.

"I think that's enough," Cinthia, one of the girls holding Nichelle said, after Lerrick landed a few more punches. But, Lerrick was consumed with jealousy and blurred of all reasonable thinking, to the point that it was evident that Nichelle was in a great deal of physical pain, the type of pain that ran much deeper than punches to her face.

"Yo, I'm outta here! You taking this shit too far!" Kyla, the other girl said, getting panicky. Both girls let Nichelle go and she fell to the floor.

"Come on, Lerrick, let's go! She ain't lookin' too good."

"Ya'll some punks! Go head and leave. I ain't done yet."

"You buggin'…we out!" Cinthia and Kyla took off running, leaving Nichelle and Lerrick alone.

"I guess it's just you and me now."

"Lerrick, please!" Nichelle cried out, trying to stand up.

"Shut the fuck up!" she barked, lifting her Timberland boot back with all her might and stomping Nichelle in her stomach three times.

Nichelle screamed out in pain as she held her midsection.

"Now, I'm done," Lerrick snickered. "Shit, I got your nasty ass vomit on my hand from roughing up your face. I bet you don't feel pretty anymore," she continued, walking over to the sink to wash her hands.

Nichelle's excruciating pain had quickly turned to pure contempt. Seeing the pleasure on Lerrick's face was all the motivation she needed to set shit straight.

Lerrick was so busy gloating over her so-called victory, she didn't even see the wrath of Nichelle coming until her blood gushed across the mirror. Lerrick's heart almost stopped beating from the shock of witnessing the entire right side of her face slashed open from the slicing Nichelle did with her razor.

"I pray you see me in your nightmares!" Nichelle uttered, in a haunting tone, leaving her enemy in the bathroom begging for help.

"Make sure that nigga pay you every fuckin' dime before you let him re-up on anything, you understand?" Renny towered over one of his street soldiers, burning through his eyes, making sure he was grasping each word coming out his mouth.

"On everything...I got you. I won't front that nigga shit else until he all paid up."

"No, motherfucker, even after this nigga no longer got a negative balance, you ain't frontin' him shit. We don't front our product."

"Oh, Radric used to let me front the nigga because he buy a lot of product from us and he always been loyal. This the latest he ever been paying up."

"Radric was my man, and God bless his soul, but

he ain't wit' us no longer, so I run these projects now. And the frontin' policy is dead," Renny said, crossing his arms over his chest. "Business tactics like that is how your money get fucked up. Kasaun, if you don't learn nothing else from me, remember this. Don't neva let nothing leave your hand unless the person you're giving it to is putting something right back in it. You give a motherfucker some drugs, they pay what they owe right then...it's as simple as that. I hope we're clear."

As the young soldier nodded his head and continued talking, trying to convince Renny he understood everything he said, the ice-blue Benz speeding down the street caught his attention.

"We good, Kasaun, I'll speak to you tomorrow," Renny said, rushing dude off. He recognized the car being the one he saw Nichelle driving at Carmelo's funeral. He quickly walked across the street towards a parking lot when he saw her pull in. When he got closer, he saw Nichelle getting out the car. He waited to see what direction she was going, and she crossed the street coming to the side he was standing on.

Nichelle's head was down, but when she walked past him, Renny made his move. "Hey, don't I know you. Isn't your name Nichelle?" he asked casually.

Nichelle quickly glanced up, "No, you don't." She then quickly looked right back down, not wanting to make eye contact.

But Renny saw enough of her face to know something was wrong. "Nichelle, what happened to you?" He reached for her arm and held it.

His concern sounded so authentic, that Nichelle couldn't help but turn around and look him in the eyes. "Do I know?" she stared intently. "Oh yeah, I met you at Carmelo's funeral," she said, immediately recognizing his face once she took the time to look.

"Yes. But I want to know who did this to you?" Renny felt a sort of anger smoldering inside him that had him somewhat taken aback.

"I really need to go and lay down. I'm not feeling too good."

"You live around here?"

"Yes, in the building right over there." Nichelle pointed to one of the projects that Renny now had on lock.

"I'll walk you home," he stated, still holding on to her arm.

"You don't have to do that for me."

"Yes, I do." It was obvious somebody had fucked Nichelle up pretty badly, and Renny didn't think she was in any condition to be alone. He honestly wanted to pick her up and carry her to his crib so he could take care of her. She looked so helpless to him, like a wounded puppy.

"Oh, God!" Nichelle murmured as a sharp pain shot through her stomach. She felt a wet warmness in her panties, and when she looked down, she could see blood seeping through her gray jogging pants.

"Come over here and sit down," Renny directed. When he held her arm, about to guide her over to the bench, he saw the blood. At first he thought maybe she had unexpectedly started her period, but with a bruised face and the way she was holding her stomach, he figured it was something much worse than that. "Come on, I'm taking you to the hospital."

Renny lifted Nichelle off her feet and carried her down the street until he got to his truck. He laid her across the back seat, and he was worried because it seemed as if she was going in and out of consciousness. He also heard her mumbling something, but he couldn't make out what she was saying. But he put all that out his head and focused on getting her to the emergency room.

Renny fought his way through traffic headed, towards the nearest hospital. Every chance he got, he would glance in the backseat to keep tabs on how Nichelle was holding up, and it wasn't looking good, but at least her eyes were open.

"Move your fuckin' car and drive!" Renny roared out the window and blew his horn at a car in front of him. The couple was so busy arguing with each other that they weren't aware that the light had turned green. "Hold on, Nichelle, we're almost there," Renny called out when he was a few blocks away from the hospital. But, this time when he turned around to check on her, she was as motionless as a dead person.

"I'm surprised to see you home so early," Tierra's mom said when she came in the kitchen.

"It was Nichelle's first day back at school since what happened to Carmello and Simone, and I wanted to check on her. I stopped by, but she must didn't get home from school yet."

"I still can't believe Simone is gone. I ran into her mother at the corner store yesterday. She had her grandson, and I swear that little boy looks just like Simone. I know it must break her heart every time she looks at his sweet face."

"I know," Tierra sighed, sitting down at the small round table.

"I bet you the cops ain't got no leads."

"Nope."

"Why, when it come to 'hood crimes the cops can't never figure shit out? But if Simone was some white girl from one of those ritzy neighborhoods, that shit would be on 'Nancy Grace' every damn day. They'd have a ton of pictures plastered from the time she was a baby, until the day she died. When is these young black people gon' realize that they are an endangered species?"

"I don't know," Tierra shrugged, not in the mood for one of her mother's sermons.

"Well, you better figure it out real soon, or that might be you being buried next time. A bullet ain't got no name written on it," she continued as she washed dishes. "I bet my life that whatever lowlife came and shot them people, Simone was not the intended target. She just happened to be at the wrong place at the wrong time."

"So what? I'm supposed to stop living my life because of what happened to Simone?"

"Damn straight, if you want to see thirty! Hell, make it another day, at the rate these heartless bastards is taking innocent people out this world. You need to stop running around with these hooligans and get a job, be productive."

"So what, I can bust my ass working multiple jobs and barely be able to pay my bills like you?"

Tierra's mother put down the bowl in her hand and turned off the faucet. "Listen here. I may not be rolling in the money like them misguided poison pushers you affiliate with, but I sleep easy every night when I go to bed. The only person who sometimes keeps me awake at night from worrying, is you. We lost your father to these streets, and I don't want to lose you too."

"You want me to give up on wanting a better life for myself. I don't get it. You used to be so full of life. I remember when I was a little girl and you would get dressed up and go out with daddy, I was in awe of you. You were the most beautiful woman I had ever seen. I wanted to look and be just like you when I grew up."

"You're not a little girl anymore, and it's time for you to get your head out the clouds and face reality. What's the sense of being beautiful if you're dead?"

"I'm sorry, but I want more out of life, and these streets is gonna help me get it."

"Well then, I better start making your funeral arrangements now, since it's more important to you that you're able to live your life reckless so you can die beautiful," she reasoned, throwing her towel down and leaving the kitchen, unable to bear being in the same room with her daughter any longer.

Scared Of
Lonely

When true love is lost, is it possible to rebirth it with someone else, or are you only trying to re-ignite a flame that has permanently died out? For many, taking another chance at love only to risk being burned again is a chance they aren't willing to take. But for the few who are keen on taking the gamble, the reward may pay out more than you could've ever anticipated.

When Nichelle woke up, she dreaded opening her eyes to the same lifeless white walls that held her captive less than two weeks ago. But when she turned her head, a man who she had to admit was extremely handsome, was sitting in a chair with the most concerned expression, adorning his face.

"You're awake. Are you feeling better?"

"Much better. How long have I been here?"

"A few hours."

"Have you been sitting there the whole time?"

"Yes, and I was prepared to stay cemented in this chair until you woke up."

"Oh God, my baby!" Nichelle said in a panic,

laying her hand on her stomach, not thinking about anything else.

"I'm sorry, Nichelle, but the baby didn't make it."

"How do you know?" she asked, as her lips trembled.

"When I brought you in, the doctor and nurses assumed I was the father, so they told me."

Nichelle put her head down in defeat. "I can't believe I lost Carmelo's baby! This child was all I had left of him!"

"That's not true. He may be dead, but he's still with you in spirit."

Nichelle looked up, meeting Renny's glare. "I would've never pegged you as the spiritual type."

"Thugs can be deep too."

"True. Carmelo was one of the deepest people I knew." Renny was already sick of hearing Carmelo's name, but he understood Nichelle was very much in love with the man, so it was to be expected.

"Not to change the subject, but you never told me who did this to you."

"This trife chick named Lerrick I go to school wit'. I told that bitch I was pregnant too, and she still kicked me in my stomach!"

"Lerrick…what's her last name? Because she has to be dealt with."

"No need. My signature has been permanently engraved on that raggedy heffa's face. But that won't bring back my baby. I had mentally started making so many plans for a child I'll never see. How dumb was that?"

"There's nothing dumb about it. What's dumb is some stupid broad robbed you of those plans. You can never replace the baby you lost, but try to take some comfort in knowing you can have another one."

"You're right. And hopefully, next time the father will be around to share in the joy with me."

"He will."

"I've been talking to you all this time, and I don't even know your name, or maybe you did tell me and I can't remember. Regardless, tell me, because this time I won't forget it."

"Renny O'Neal."

"Thank you, Renny, for thinking enough of me to bring me to the hospital instead of leaving me on the corner where you saw me."

"It's not even in me to be that careless about another person's life. But you're welcome, and I hope you get better soon."

"Are you leaving me?" Renny could detect the fear in her voice and on her face when he stood up. "I shouldn't have asked you that."

"Why not?"

"Because, bringing me to the hospital is more than most people would do, and I'm sure you've *been* ready to go. I mean, you have more important things to do then sit in a hospital room, keeping a girl company that you hardly know."

"Actually, I would like to keep you company."

"Seriously?"

"I don't have anything to do for the rest of the evening. Besides starving, I'm good." Renny managed to get a slight laugh out of Nichelle, which was a difficult task under the circumstances. "Can I bring you anything back?"

"No, I don't have much of an appetite, but thanks."

"I'll be back shortly."

"Hurry." Nichelle did want Renny to hurry back. She was at a place in her life where she was scared of lonely. Everybody she loved was taken out of her life. From watching the only man she knew as a father die at the hands of her mother, to Carmelo being murdered, and now her unborn child, she felt lost and was desperate for a savior.

"Miss Martin."

Nichelle stepped out her gloomy thoughts when the nurse came in.

"Yes."

"I don't know if your boyfriend told you—"

"Oh, he's not my boyfriend," Nichelle quickly said, cutting the nurse off.

"I apologize. He seemed so concerned about you, I assumed he was your boyfriend."

"He did?"

"Yes, very concerned. He refused to leave your side. He must care about you a great deal."

To Nichelle's surprise, hearing that gave her this funny tingling feeling inside.

"But what he couldn't tell us, was what happened to you. How did you get all those bruises on your face and there was bruising on your stomach?"

Nichelle thought about what the nurse asked her,

and whether or not she should tell her it was Lerrick's jealous ass. But no matter how much she detested Lerrick, Nichelle wasn't a snitch. She would rather get street justice, which she already did, than ever fuck with the police.

"I was walking home from school and some girls ran up behind me and tried to rob me. I tried to fight back, but as you can see, they got the best of me."

"Did you see their faces? Do you know who it was?"

"Nope. All I was trying to do was hold on to my purse, which I did."

"A purse isn't worth your life. I need to call the police so you can file a report."

"Report what? I didn't even get to see their faces. I was too busy tryna block punches. You know the cops ain't gon' do nothing anyway. They can't close cases even when they got witnesses."

The nurse shook her head, too tired from working double shifts to argue with Nichelle. "What I came to tell you is, the doctor wants you to stay overnight for observation."

"Am I okay?"

"You should be fine. But, you lost a significant amount of blood when you miscarried, so the doctor wants to monitor you, to be on the safe side. If you need anything, just push the button."

"I will." When the nurse left, Nichelle called her mother so she wouldn't worry when she didn't come home.

"Hello."

"Hey, it's me, Nichelle."

"Hi, baby. I just walked in from work. How was your first day back at school?"

"Not good."

"What happened?"

"I'll talk to you about it when I get home tomorrow."

"Why aren't you coming home until tomorrow?"

"Because I'm at the hospital."

"What! Nichelle, what happened? What hospital are you at, because I'm coming up there!"

"Don't, please! I'm gonna be fine. They just wanna keep me here for observation. Don't worry, I'll be home tomorrow. But, I want to be alone right now."

"Nichelle, what is really going on with you?" Her mother's voice had gone from being alarmed, to straight pissed that her daughter was laid up in the hospital again, but wanted to be so vague about why she was there.

"Ma, I have to go. I'll call you tomorrow," Nichelle said, quickly hanging up the phone when Renny came in.

"You didn't have to hang up with your mother because of me."

"I didn't. She was asking me a bunch of questions I wasn't in the mood to answer. I'm glad you came back, but visiting hours are gonna be over soon. I wish I could leave with you, but the doctor wants me to stay overnight."

"It's understandable. You looked real bad when you came in here. I know they must've thought I was some abusive boyfriend that fucked you up."

"No, the nurse said you seemed to really care about me."

"I do."

"Why? You don't even know me."

"When I say this, I don't want you to think I'm some crazy guy you should be afraid of."

"I would never think that. If you hadn't helped me, I could be a lot worse off than I am right now. You probably saved my life."

"I wouldn't go that far."

"The nurse told me I lost a lot of blood. I never paid a lot of attention in school, but I do remember learning that losing too much blood leads to death. So, say what you were about to tell me, and I promise I won't think you're crazy."

"Remember you said that."

"Would you say it already?"

"This is gonna sound soft but it's true...I've had a thing for you since the first time I saw you."

"You mean at Carmelo's funeral?"

"No, months ago, when Radric and I came to pick up Tierra and Simone."

"Where was this?"

"You came to Simone's house to baby-sit so she could go out."

"Oh, yeah, Tierra had called me at the last minute. But, I don't remember seeing you there that day."

"I was in Radric's car. You didn't see me, but I saw you. I can't lie, I was diggin' your physical beauty, but it was something about the way you held Simone's baby that drew me in. You seemed so innocent. I think that's why when I saw you on the street looking fucked up and in pain, I was fuckin' fuming. I didn't understand how anybody could hurt you like that."

"I don't know what to say."

"I knew you were gonna think I was crazy."

"Definitely not. If anything, I'm surprised. As cute as you are, you can have any chick you want. I can't believe you were checkin' for me like that."

"You mean that shit too, and that's what makes you appear so innocent, 'cause you don't even know how fine you are. For me, that turns me on even more. I run into broads all day that don't even register a five on a scale of one through ten, but you can't tell them they ain't the coldest thing walking the streets."

"That's funny!" Nichelle couldn't help but laugh at his candidness.

"No, that shit ain't funny, it's a fuckin' nightmare, 'cause there's a lot of delusional broads runnin' around here. But yo, back to you. I didn't tell you what I did to put any pressure on you. I know you been through a lot, losing your man, friend, and the miscarriage. But I wanted to tell you how I felt, and if nothin' comes of it, I hope we can at least be friends."

"I want that too—I mean the friendship part. Honestly, right now I can't think about tryna be in a relationship with somebody else. My heart belongs to Carmelo."

"I respect that. But, um, it's getting late. I better head out."

"You are coming back tomorrow?"

"Do you want me to?"

"Yes," Nichelle admitted, nodding her head.

"Then I'll be here. Get some rest."

A devilish grin crept across Renny's face after he left Nichelle's room. She wasn't ready yet, but eventually he was positive she would be his. He sincerely felt bad about what happened to Nichelle, but he also believed it was divine intervention that made it possible for him to be the one to save her. And he planned to fully use it to his advantage.

Contagious

If you maintain long enough in the game, at some point you reach a pinnacle. It's the point where you've stacked enough paper, balled until you're about to fall, flossed so ridiculously that your iconic status is forever engraved in the minds of the streets you ran. To the few that reach that level, it's no longer about the need to help your people who are indigent. It becomes about your addicition to the chase. But be careful what you keep chasing after, whether it is money or women, because both can lead to a dead end street.

Arnez watched from the back seat of his car as Talisa came out of the high-rise apartment she shared with Genesis that was until he disappeared. Now, he was on the run from the Feds, and yet she stayed put, instead of going back home to her family in New York.

"Arnez, every other day you're out here in this car watching her. What is the point?" Chanel wanted to know.

"I'm waiting for her to lead me to Genesis."

"Then what?"

"So I can kill him, of course."

"You want that bitch back, don't you? You think after you kill Genesis, Talisa will come running back to you? Doubt it!"

"Watch your mouth, Chanel!"

Arnez kept his glare on Talisa and observed as she looked around briefly before getting in her car. "Follow her," he directed his driver.

The driver steadily but discreetly trailed behind Talisa's black Aston Martin as she maneuvered through the streets of Philly for about fifteen minutes, until pulling into an outdoor parking lot. Talisa got out the car, signaling the alarm before heading into a nondescript brick building.

"Max, go find out what type of building that is," Arnez ordered his driver to do, after waiting a few minutes to make sure Talisa wasn't coming right back outside.

"Yes, Mr. Douglass." The driver ran across the street and went inside the building. A few minutes later, he came back out and got in the car. "It's an OBGYN, Sir."

"Is Talisa pregnant? If so, could the baby be mine, or is that motherfucker, Genesis the father?" Arnez asked out loud as Chanel cringed in her seat. "Drive," Arnez told his driver as he lit up a cigarette.

"So what now, Arnez?" Chanel questioned, in an icy tone.

"I find out if the baby Talisa is carrying is mine."

"What if it is?"

"Then Talisa and the baby can live. If not..." His

voice faded off, but Chanel knew how the sentence was supposed to end, and she prayed it wasn't his. She was tired of living in Talisa's shadow. She had lied, cheated, and turned on her own sister for Arnez, but yet, he continued to stalk a woman that wanted nothing to do with him.

On several occasions, Chanel considered putting a bullet through Talisa and getting rid of the competition permanently, but knew Arnez would kill her if he ever found out. She was also sure that he probably had one of his men watching Talisa's every move, so the chances of getting away with it were slim to none. But if it did turn out that Talisa was pregnant and Arnez was the father, Chanel knew her relationship with him would never go any further than what it was right now. Forever being his bottom bitch wasn't a position Chanel intended to keep playing. She was prepared to do anything necessary to not only be the main, but the only bitch in his life… period!

"I know you ain't still sleep like you want to stay in this cold ass hospital room another day," Renny said, when he entered Nichelle's room.

"No, I'm up," she answered, turning around in her bed to face him. Her eyes widened when she saw he hadn't come empty handed. "What's all that?"

"Some flowers to celebrate your release, and a change of clothes, unless you tryna put back on what you came in."

"Hell no! I was hoping they burned those clothes. That was very considerate of you. I had so much on my mind, I forgot all about what I was going to wear home."

"That's what you got me for. I hope they fit a'ight, but I'm usually pretty good at sizing up a woman's measurements," he said, handing Nichelle the bag with the clothes in them.

"I'm sure you are. Oh, and the flowers are beautiful. Do you know you're the first guy that has given me flowers? Carmelo never even did that. Wow, that's crazy."

"That is surprising, but I'm sure he made up for that in other ways."

"Yeah, he did, but having you bring me some makes me realize how nice it is. Thank you."

"You welcome. Now get dressed. I'm sure you're ready to get outta here, and honestly, I ain't neva liked hospitals. So the sooner we bounce, the better."

"I'm with you."

"Cool. I'll be waiting out in the hall."

"Renny," Nichelle called out as he was leaving.

"What's up?"

"I really do appreciate you being so nice to me."

"I know," he smiled and left.

When Nichelle got out the bed to go to the bathroom, her body was still aching from the beating Lerrick put on her. All the events from the last week or so had her completely drained—emotionally and physically. She turned the light on in the bathroom, and the very sight of her face made her want to scream.

She didn't understand how Renny could even stand looking at her. Her whole face appeared to be swollen.

"I can't walk out this hospital with my face looking like this. I would scare the shit out of people. Damn, I wish I had a hat to put on. At least that would cover me up somewhat," Nichelle thought out loud as she examined herself in the mirror.

Then she opened up the bag and pulled out a red velour sweatsuit Renny got her, and noticed that he not only bought a new pair of sneakers for her, but also a baseball cap and some sunglasses. Her insides lit up.

"It's like he read my mind," she said, taking off the hospital gown.

When she finished getting dressed, she didn't look like her regular self, but she felt way better than when she first looked at herself in the mirror.

"Not bad. I didn't do bad at all," Renny commented when Nichelle came out.

"I think you did pretty good. The sweatsuit fits right, and better than that, you brought me a hat and some sunglasses to cover my face. Thank you."

"I want you to know I brought you that, not because I have a problem looking at your face, because you still beautiful to me. But I know women can be self conscious about their appearance, and I didn't want to make shit uncomfortable for you."

As Nichelle walked out the hospital with Renny, a feeling of guiltiness swept through her. She had just lost who she considered the love of her life, but at the same time, she couldn't front. She was already feeling another man. She was trying her best not to acknowledge it, but it was becoming increasingly harder for her to deny. It was as if his swagger was contagious. She glanced over at Renny, and dude was straight up fine. Then, he was such a gentleman. He conducted himself in the kind of way that you only heard or saw in movies and shit.

I mean, Nichelle wasn't completely naive. It was clear to her that with all the kindness he had been showering her with, that he also had a very dark side. It wasn't obvious, but the eyes never lie. Through the calm exterior, there was so much more brewing underneath.

"Am I dropping you off at the same spot I saw you yesterday?" Renny asked when they got to his car.

"Yeah, I guess," Nichelle said, getting in the car.

"I thought I remember your girl telling me and Radric a while back that you lived in Long Island," Renny inquired, already knowing what had gone down, but wanting to get some feedback on the situation from Nichelle.

"I did, before Carmelo died. But I had to leave," she answered earnestly.

"Damn, the building management made you leave so soon? That was cold!"

"It wasn't exactly the building management."

"Then who? 'Cause real talk, the building management can't just throw you out on the street like that, whether homeboy died or not. There is a legal procedure they got to go through."

"So I heard, but after what I found out, I didn't

want to be there anymore anyway."

"If you don't mind me asking, what did you find out?"

Nichelle hesitated for a minute, but she was feeling at ease around Renny and wanted to discuss what had happened to her with somebody else, besides Tierra.

"I feel embarrassed to admit this, but it is what it is. Carmelo was married."

"What!" Renny played it perfectly, like it was new news to him. "I can't believe that nigga was married! But you ain't got no reason to be embarrassed. You ain't do nothing wrong. That was on him."

"Then why do I feel like it's my fault, like somehow I'm the blame for him lying to me all that time?"

"Because you're a sweet person, Nichelle. Instead of putting the blame on others, you'd much rather put it on yourself."

"That's crazy you say that, because that's so true."

"How did you find out?" again, he already knew the answer, but continued the charade.

"His wife showed up after the funeral and told me."

"That must've been hard."

"It was devastating! She shattered damn near every idea I had about the love Carmelo and I shared."

"That man might've fucked up, but trust, he loved you."

Nichelle turned her entire body around in the passenger seat and stared at Renny. "You really think so?" She yearned to believe that.

"I know so. I saw you together a couple of times, and trust, I know when a man loves a woman. And Carmelo definitely loved you."

"Tierra told me the same thing, but hearing that from another man makes it seem more believable." The fact that Renny didn't bash Carmelo like Nichelle thought most men would do, especially one that admitted he liked her, made her find him more attractive. Renny was no fool. He figured that would be the exact affect it would have on her.

"I am sorry you had to get put out your crib like that. His wife didn't have to come so hard at you, but then again, she probably was bitter, which is understandable too."

"Yeah, that's how I felt. Tierra thought I should stay just to fuck wit' her, but that's not my style."

"I can tell, and it's another quality that makes you appealing."

"You gon' stop wit' all the compliments! You gon' make my already swollen face get even bigger."

"I doubt I can do that," he joked.

"Forget you!" Nichelle said, playfully hitting Renny on the arm. Then she hissed and sat back in the seat.

"What's wrong?" It was visible to Renny that something had quickly upset her.

"I don't want to go home yet."

"What, you hungry? You want me to stop and get you something to eat?"

"I mean, I don't want to go back to my mothers'

and stay there. She's gon' grill the shit out of me when she sees my face. Then to tell her about the miscarriage and all that other shit, I ain't ready for all that."

"Do you want me to take you to a friend's place?"

"Tierra is the only friend I have, and we live in the same building. A lot of times she acts more like my mother than a friend, so I don't feel like seeing her either."

"So, where do you want me to take you? If you want, I can get you a room at a hotel for however long you like."

"Thanks, but I don't want to be alone."

"Do you want to stay with me for a couple of days? I have a couple extra bedrooms, and I promise not to interfere on your space."

"You really wouldn't mind? I mean, I know you probably have a lot of women that you be entertaining. I wouldn't want to cramp your style."

"I don't entertain women at my crib. I prefer to maintain my privacy."

"So why are you letting me stay?"

"Because I know you're going through a rough time, and I consider us friends. This ain't 'bout no entertaining'."

Nichelle sat back in the seat and thought about what Renny said. She wasn't sure if she liked being called just his friend. Then her mind began wondering about the type of women he would entertain, how they looked, and where he did the entertaining, since it wasn't at his crib.

As Renny crossed over the George Washington

Bridge, headed to New Jersey, she realized that all the things she shouldn't care about in regards to Renny's personal life, she found herself deliberating on it.

"Hey, Ms. Martin," did Nichelle leave for school yet?"

"No, you haven't spoken to her?"

"Not since early yesterday. Why, where is she?"

"The hospital. I'm surprised she didn't call you."

"The hospital! What happened? Is she alright?" Tierra instantly thought about the baby Nichelle was carrying, and wondered if that had anything to do with it. She didn't want to say too much though, because she wasn't sure if Nichelle had confided in her mother about the pregnancy yet.

"Your guess is as good as mine. When she called last night, she wouldn't tell me nothing."

"What hospital is she at?"

"I don't know. She wouldn't say, and I didn't even bother to call around and ask. She told me she was fine, and begged me not to come and see her, so I let it be. When Nichelle is ready, she'll tell me what happened."

"You ain't worried?"

"Of course I'm worried! But Nichelle is eighteen years old. One thing I've learned over the years, is that when somebody wants to be left alone, give them their space."

"Will she be home today?"

"Supposed to be."

"I hope so, because I really need to speak to her."

"Did you try her cell?"

"Yeah, but it keeps going straight to voice mail."

"Again, she don't want to be bothered, so let her be. When Nichelle's ready, she'll be back. Until then, all I can do is keep her in my prayers."

"I hear you. If you talk to her before me, please tell her to give me a call."

"I will, Tierra. You take care now," Ms. Martin said, closing the door.

Tierra wished her mother could be more like Nichelle's mom—laid back and not preachy. She felt her mother would never respect her wishes and give her space if she needed it. Instead, she would give her a sermon about all the things she was doing wrong, and what to do to make it right. But Tierra hoped that she would be escaping the constant lectures from her mother in the near future. She had done her part on the proposition that was offered to her, and soon planned on cashing in.

Your Time Is Up

Loyalty in the streets can be a dicey call. When it's all lovely for everybody in the crew, the allegiance seems intact. But the second one of its members comes under attack, that's when the cracks begin to show.

"Damn, yo', your face is fucked up! Nichelle did a number on you!" Kyla commented to Lerrick as they sat in White Castle.

"It looks better than it did when you first got the stitches," Cinthia said, trying to make Lerrick feel a little bit better.

"That's a'ight, Nichelle may have fucked my face up, but when I get done wit' her, her own mother won't even be able to recognize her."

"Lerrick, I know you ain't still gon' fuck wit' her. I think it's best you let it go, especially since you were the one who started it anyway. If you would've left when Cinthia and I broke out, we wouldn't even be having this conversation."

"Fuck that!" Lerrick flung her arm, knocking her

hamburger off the table. "I have to walk around for the rest of my life wit' this scar on my face! Ain't no way I'ma let that snobby bitch get away wit' this!"

"Lerrick, you know you my girl, but I might have to agree wit' Kyla on this one. Maybe you should let it go. She looked real bad when we left her on that bathroom floor, then homegirl said she was pregnant too. Maybe that's why ain't nobody seen her, 'cause she damn sure ain't been in school. What if she lost the baby?" Cinthia's voice went low, and she glanced around the table, shaking her head nervously.

"That bitch was lying. She wasn't pregnant, and I don't give a fuck if she was! Nichelle can't hide forever. Soon she gon' have to show her face, and when she do, I'll be waiting to attack that ass!"

What was supposed to have been a couple days of Nichelle hiding out at Renny's house quickly turned into a few weeks. But it was understandable why Nichelle was finding it so difficult to leave. From the moment the private elevator took them from the garage to the top floor, she started tripping. She thought she was living beyond good at the condo she shared with Carmelo, but in comparison to the townhouse Renny called home, they had been slumming it.

Nichelle had never even known cribs like this existed. The four bedrooms, three and a half bathroom domain was spectacular, to say the least. It had direct southeast views of the Hudson River and the Manhattan skyline. Even though she didn't know how to cook, when she walked into the kitchen, it made her want to learn how. It had custom cherry cabinetry with opaque glass fronts, a granite countertop island and flooring, onyx mosaic back splash, and of course, top-of-the-line stainless steel appliances.

The three-level staircases were granite and marble, with marble floors in the great room, dining room and family room. The upper level had bamboo flooring, and the lower level had a home theater. The hotness of the crib was almost too much for Nichelle to take in.

"I know you're ready for me to leave," Nichelle said, as she sat at the kitchen table eating a bowl of Cap'n Crunch, Crunch Berries cereal.

Renny sat across from her at the table reading the *Wall Street Journal* like he did every morning, and ignored her for a few minutes. For the past week, she would make the same statement, only for Renny to pacify her. This time it would be different.

"You're right. I am ready for you to go. Hurry up and get your things together so I can take you home," he answered, not moving his eyes away from the newspaper.

Nichelle dropped her spoon, and the milk and cereal splashed on the glass top.

"I'm so sorry!" Nichelle jumped up and retrieved some paper towels and wet them to clean up the mess she made. The shock of hearing Renny's reply to what she said made her whole body jump. "After I finish cleaning up this mess, I'll get dressed so you can take me back to Queens."

Renny looked over his newspaper on the sly, and could see the sadness on Nichelle's face as she steadily kept wiping the same spot that was already clean. "I was fuckin' wit' you! You know I don't want you to leave."

"Yes, you do. You're only saying that now because you feel sorry for me."

"Nichelle, I'm serious. It was a joke. Every day it's the same routine, you make that statement, and I always tell you, you're good. But it's like you don't believe me, so I wanted to cure you from that shit. So, do we have a deal? Will you stop asking me that same bullshit question? If I wanted you gone, I would've helped you get your shit together and took you home... believe me!"

During the time Nichelle had been around Renny, it was true that he wasn't one to hold back his thoughts. If he didn't approve of something, he was quick to let you know. Nichelle got a small dose of it on the second day she was there. While touring the three-level townhouse, she came across a room on the top floor with the door closed. Thinking nothing of it, she opened the door and was about to turn on the light when Renny walked up on her. He didn't ask her any questions, he simply told her to close the door. And in a very calm, cool, collective manner, he said that she was welcome to make herself comfortable in any room in the house, except for that one, and to never go in there again. His direct, no-nonsense approach would make even the boldest person back down and follow his directions.

"I do believe you. I guess what it is, is that I'm not ready to leave. But then who would want to leave a place like this?" she smiled, admiring her surroundings.

"So what, you want to move in permanently?"

The question caught Nichelle so completely off guard that she didn't know how to respond. "Is this a trick question?" she finally asked.

"The only trick is what your answer is gonna be," Renny laughed. "Living in Edgewater, New Jersey is a big difference than Queens. You have to think about being away from your family and friends."

"Besides my mom and Tierra, there ain't nothing left for me in Queens. My mother's always working, so I hardly saw her anyway and Tierra, we can still hangout sometimes. And it's not like I would stay here forever, just until I got my mind right."

"Is that a 'yes'?"

"Of course it's a 'yes', as long as you're cool with it."

"Good, but I only have one stipulation."

"I knew it. So what do you want from me?" Nichelle wouldn't admit it to Renny, but she hoped the stipulation would be that she had to stop sleeping in one of his guest bedrooms and give him some pussy. Since she'd been there, Renny hadn't so much as tried to kiss her, and it had made her want him even more. When Ne-Yo had said it was the year of the gentleman, Renny was it. He had provided her with clothes, food, and shelter, not asking her for shit in return. Now he had a stipulation, and Nichelle wanted it to be one where she could show him how grateful she was for all his generosity.

"I want you to finish high school. You're a senior with only a few months until you graduate. If you want to stay here, you have to finish school."

Nichelle put her head down and sighed. "I don't want to go back there."

"Why not?"

"For one, do you know how early I would have to get up to get to school everyday?"

"Anything worth having, you have to make sacrifices. It's only a few more months, Nichelle."

"Plus, I'm so far behind on my schoolwork I'll never be able to catch up."

"Enough with the excuses. You see this newspaper I'm reading?" Renny asked, holding up the *Wall Street Journal*. "I read this every day so I can know what the fuck is going on in corporate America, because believe it or not, this shit dictates a lot of what's poppin' off in the streets. Knowledge really is fuckin' power, and being a dumbass will never get you any fuckin' where in life. If I didn't think you had potential to make something out of your life, I would tell you to drop out and work for me doing some street dirt. But, you're better than that."

"How do you know?"

"Because I read some of the poems and short stories you've written since you've been here."

"You went in my room?"

"No, the other night when you fell asleep in the theater room, your notebook was open on the chair next to you, and I read it. There were some powerful words in there. But you need your education."

"I don't know, Renny. I have so many bad memories at that school. I don't know if I can go back."

"Yes, you can, and you will."

She looked up at him, and it was difficult to tell a man like him 'no'.

"Okay, I'll go back, but since it's Thursday, and the week is about over, can I start on Monday?"

"Yes."

"Can you take me to Queens over the weekend so I can stop home and get some clothes and my car?"

"I tell you what. We can go to the mall here in Jersey and get you some clothes for school, and I'll drive you to school Monday. After I pick you up, we can stop by your crib to get whatever you need, and your car."

"Whatever you say."

"Good. I have to head out, but I'll be back later on tonight. Call me if you need anything."

Nichelle did need something, and his name was Renny O'Neal. It blew her mind how she went from crying over Carmelo, to dreaming about falling asleep in Renny's arms. But she felt like the tables had turned, and Renny was no longer sexually attracted to her, and only thought of her as a pet project he needed to salvage. Now that she found herself falling for him, she no longer wanted to be *just friends*. She craved so much more.

Knock... Knock...Knock

"Who is it?"

"It's me, Ms. Martin," Tierra said, starting to feel like a stalker.

"Just a minute." Tierra could hear Ms. Martin, unbolting the lock and chain so she could open the door. "Good morning, Tierra, and no, Nichelle ain't come home yet."

"Have you spoken to her again?"

"Yes, she called a few days ago."

"Did you tell her I said to call me?"

"Yes, I did, but I assume she still hasn't called you. I'm sorry, but I think she's going through a rough time and wants to be left alone. She won't even tell me where or who she's staying with. The only reason she's probably calling me is so I know she's safe, and I don't file a missing person report."

"I don't understand why she hasn't called me. Next time you speak to her, tell her to please call. Tell her I won't ask her a whole bunch of questions, I just want to know how she's doing."

"I will, Tierra. I don't mean to rush you off, but I have to get ready for work. You take care now."

No more than five minutes after Ms. Martin closed the door and started to get dressed, she heard the phone ringing. "Hello."

"Hey, Ma, it's me."

"Baby, how are you?"

"Okay. I'm coming home Monday."

"For good, I hope."

"No. I'm coming to get some clothes and my car.

180

I'm gonna stay where I've been for a little while longer, but I am going back to school."

"It's good to hear you're going back to school, but why ain't you coming home, and who are you staying with?"

"Where I am, it's better for me...no drama. But, if you're home on Monday after I get out of school, maybe you can meet the person I'm staying with, and you'll feel more at ease."

"I haven't seen you in weeks Nichelle. I'll be here Monday."

"Okay. I love you, and I'll see you then."

"Love you too...oh wait, Nichelle!" Ms. Martin yelled out, trying to catch Nichelle before she hung up the phone.

"Yes?"

"Tierra left here a few minutes ago, looking for you again. Please call her, she's worried about you and I'm tired of her knocking on my door every other day to see if I spoke to you."

"Okay, I'll call her today."

"You promise?"

"Yes, I promise."

"Good. See you on Monday."

As Tierra walked to the beauty salon, she was still pissed about her conversation with Ms. Martin. It angered her that Nichelle had gone missing, and hadn't bothered to call her. They were supposed to be best friends. And not only that, Tierra was concerned about her pregnancy. She wanted to make sure that she and the baby were alright. With each passing day, Tierra was becoming more worried, but she decided she would figure out what to do later, because right now, she had to get her hair done.

"Hey, Charlene," Tierra waved to her hairdresser when she walked in. For a Thursday morning, it was already packed, but Tierra remembered it was the first of the month, and everybody was spending their checks.

"Hey, girl, have a seat. I'll be done in a few minutes."

Tierra sat down while Charlene put the finishing touches on a weave. She noticed the *Vibe* Magazine with Kanye West on the cover in the seat next to her, and decided to pick it up. It was then that she saw Kay Kay getting up from under the dryer. Tierra decided to act like she didn't see her and continue reading her magazine, because she wasn't in the mood for drama. If Kay Kay didn't say anything to her, then she would remain on mute. But of course, when Tierra heard Lerrick's name brought up, she had to listen.

"How's Lerrick's scar healing? I know the last time you were in here, you said it looked pretty bad," the stylist said, taking the rollers out of Kay Kay's hair.

"That shit ain't looking too much better. You know it's going down the entire right side of her face. Only a good plastic surgeon could make that shit look any better, and don't nobody got no money for that."

"Whoever did that shit to your sister should be

ashamed of themselves. The kids today need to stop the madness."

"It was some jealous ass bitch named Nichelle that she go to school with. Now, the bitch done went into hiding and won't show her face. She knows that Lerrick gon' beat her ass when she do."

"I wish she would! I will beat her ass like I did before if Lerrick so much as looks at Nichelle!" Tierra barked, jumping up from her chair and walking towards Kay Kay.

Kay Kay's eyes popped out, surprised to see Tierra. "What the fuck this got to do wit' you? This ain't none of your business," Kay Kay said, rolling her eyes and neck simultaneously.

"If it got to do wit' Nichelle, then it is my business. And yo' stupid ass know good and well that ain't nobody jealous of yo' busted ass sister. You up in here spreading lies about Nichelle. If she slashed Lerrick's face, best believe it was because your sister fucked wit' her first."

"You don't know what the fuck you talkin' 'bout!" "Yes, I do! Lerrick's dumb ass was fuckin' wit' Nichelle not too long ago, and I had to whip her ass like I used to do you back in ninth, tenth, eleventh and twelfth grades. So you don't know what the fuck you talkin' 'bout!"

"You ain't gon' do shit to my sister!" Kay Kay barked back, standing up from her chair.

"Bitch, sit the fuck down, before I knock the rest of them rollers out yo' head! Don't act like you don't remember how I get down!"

183

"Tierra, calm down! I don't need you destroying my salon," Charlene pleaded.

Everybody in Queens knew Tierra was a beast when it came to beating a bitch down. And for those that didn't, Tierra was quick to make them recognize.

"She don't want none of this!" Kay Kay boasted, trying her best to present a tough exterior, knowing good and well Tierra would mop up the floor with her.

"Don't worry, Charlene. I'ma have a seat and wait to get my hair done. Now you, motherfucker," Tierra turned back towards Kay Kay and pointed her finger in her direction. "I know where the fuck you live, and when I see you out in them streets, yo' monkey ass is mine…trust!"

Tierra sat back down in her chair, beyond heated. She was desperate to talk to Nichelle. *Now I understand why Nichelle went into hiding. She probably worried Lerrick is gon' retaliate against her for slashing her face. With Nichelle being pregnant, she ain't gonna wanna fight Lerrick and put the baby's life in jeopardy. So she staying out of harms way. That bitch, Lerrick got to go! Maybe then Nichelle will feel comfortable enough to come home.*

Tierra's thoughts were interrupted when she heard her cell phone ringing. "Hello."

"We need to talk. What time can we meet up?"

"Damn right we need to talk! Where you been? I've been trying to get in contact wit' you, and you been ghost."

"I've been busy, but I got something for you."

"I hope it's a lot. When I say that, I mean a lot more than we originally agreed on after the way everything went down."

"Like I said, I got you. I'll see you at the spot in say, an hour?"

"Make it two. I'm about to get my hair done."

"Two hours then, and don't be late."

Before Tierra could respond, the person on the other end hung up. But that was okay, she was finally going to collect, and that's all that mattered. She hoped that this time next week, she would be packing her shit and getting the hell out of her mom's crib.

***

"Mr. O'Neal, I hope your car meets all of your specifications," the dealer said, as Renny inspected every detail of his newly purchased Maserati Granturisimo S, at the Long Island dealership. Renny could afford any car he wanted, and had been through quite a few, but something about this particular style of vehicle gave him a hard-on. Normally he would see a car, like it and buy it. But this time he specifically selected everything from the walnut briarwood dashboard and steering wheel, the stitching matching the Rosso Corallo interior. Even the color of the brake calipers to accent the exterior and interior of the car was Renny's decision. With the executive package he had added, the car could damn near do everything but drive itself.

"This is truly my baby!" Renny glided his hand over the slick body of the car. "I can't wait to get behind the wheel," Renny smiled, to the dealer's delight.

For the last few weeks of doing business with Renny, the dealer knew how meticulous he was, and you didn't want to be in his path if something didn't meet his expectations.

"Hold on one minute, this is my other baby," he said, answering his cell. "Is everything okay?"

"Yeah, everything is fine. Are you busy?" Nichelle hardly ever called Renny. In fact, this was only the second time. She already felt that she was intruding on his personal space, so she tried not to bother him when he was out handling business.

"No, what's up?"

"I was wondering what time you were coming home. I thought maybe I could cook dinner for you."

Renny could hear the apprehension in her voice. He thought it was cute that she was feeling nervous, and he decided to fuck with her. "Nichelle, who's gonna make the food? Because you don't even know how to cook."

"How did you know? I never told you I couldn't cook!"

"You just did."

Nichelle wanted to drop the phone and hide in the closet out of embarrassment. She didn't know how to cook, but she was trying to find a way to bring some romance into the house without doing something too obvious, like opening his bedroom door, butt-ass naked.

"Nichelle, are you there?"

"I'm here."

"I have a better idea. I bought a new car today, and I can take you for a ride on our way to dinner. So be ready at eight. I'll see you then."

When he hung up, instead of Nichelle being excited that this would be their first time going out on a somewhat of a date, she felt like a complete loser. "Why in the hell did I suggest I cook him dinner? He must think I'm pathetic! He can do everything, and I can't do nothing!" She continued talking to herself out loud as she tried to straighten up his crib. She also felt that was a waste, since twice a week, he had maid service come in and clean up anyway. "What the hell does he need me for? I'm like dead weight to this dude."

Nichelle slumped down on the couch, frustrated. "Okay, he doesn't need anything from me, but he does want me to go to school. I'll do better than just go and pass, I'ma bust my ass and get excellent grades. Then I can prove to Renny that I am good at something. Yep, that's what I'll do," she decided, hoping speaking it out loud would make it come to fruition.

"Yo', this some good fuckin' weed right here!" Lerrick said, as she, Kyla and Cinthia chilled at Flushing Meadow Park.

"Look at all the stars in the sky, and the full moon. That shit is beautiful right there," Kyla said, lying on the grass, mesmerized.

"Lerrick, did you lace the weed wit' coke? 'Cause Kyla over there buggin' hard."

"Ain't nobody buggin', I'm appreciating nature."

"You might be right, Cinthia," Lerrick giggled.

"She sounding crazy. So crazy, I think it's time for us to go. It's late as hell anyway, and I got the munchies."

"Hold up, let me go piss before we break out. I won't be able to hold it until I get home."

"G'on 'head. I have a few more pulls to get off this blunt before I toss it anyway."

"You mean *we*," Cinthia clarified, making it clear she wouldn't be left out of sharing the rest of the good weed.

Kyla rushed to find a semi-private spot behind a tree, barely able to hold her urine. She struggled to unbutton and unzip her jeans, as being high was making her even clumsier. "Oh yes," she moaned, finally getting her jeans down and urinating.

When she was almost done, she was about to reach over and grab some leaves to wipe herself the best she could, but that would never happen. Without any warning, a firm hand covered her mouth, pressed her head back and slit her throat in one single stroke. The blade cut so deep, it almost severed her head. Her body was gently laid down, as to not make any noise

"Damn, Kyla, is you over there shittin' too? What the fuck is takin' you so long?" Lerrick screamed out, and then she and Cinthia laughed at the idea. "Go sneak up on her and scare the shit out of her," Lerrick whispered.

Cinthia nodded her head, letting Lerrick know she was down. Lerrick watched as Cinthia tiptoed to the tree. Cinthia kept turning back around, looking at Lerrick and covering her mouth so she wouldn't laugh out loud. But as she made her way behind the tree, Cinthia was the one in for the surprise.

By the time Cinthia saw someone dressed in all black, from the ski mask on down, the knife was already gutting out her insides. Blood spurted from her mouth as the blade went through her belly button, and then ripped up, practically snatching out both kidneys and her liver.

"Cinthia, is everything a'ight?" From where Lerrick was standing, she saw Cinthia's arm fling out in an odd manner. "Cinthia, Kyla, is everything a'ight?" This time she screamed, becoming alarmed. "This shit ain't funny! Ya' need to answer me now!"

When Lerrick saw the all black figure step from behind the tree into the moonlight, carrying a blood-drenched knife, she started hauling ass. "Oh shit! What the fuck!" she whimpered as she ran towards the highway, praying that if she made it to the wide lanes, cars would be coming by and save her. But with her being out of shape, she quickly began running out of breath. As she slowed down she could hear her attacker speeding up, getting closer and closer, until finally, her entire body fell over as her attacker lunged on top of her.

"Please don't hurt me! Please don't hurt me!" Lerrick cried out.

The attacker used every ounce of strength to keep Lerrick pinned down, and pulled a gun from a back pocket without giving her a chance to break free.

"Your time is up! This is what you and your crew get for fuckin' wit' Nichelle! Remember her name on your way to hell!" With a swift pull of the trigger, a hole was put through Lerrick's head, leaving her faceless.

I Want You To Love Me

There is nothing wrong with having great expectations. But expecting too much too fast can also push someone to make a careless move that leads to life altering repercussions.

Nichelle sat in the car silently, as Renny drove her to school. She was still livid, or more so hurt, that Renny never showed up that night to take her to dinner. By the time he got home, she had fallen asleep in her clothes, trying to wait up for him. The next morning, he apologized, but made no effort to reschedule dinner for another night.

"What time should I pick you up from school?"

"If I tell you, are you going to show up, or leave me outside waiting?"

Renny turned and glanced at Nichelle, and then put his eyes back on the road. "Is there something you want to get off your mind?" he asked, unruffled by her sassy tone.

"Why didn't you show up to take me to dinner that night?'

"I told you, I got caught up handling some business."

"Why couldn't we have gone over the weekend then?"

"We could've, but we didn't."

"Yeah, because you were barely home."

"Exactly. See, you answered your own question."

Nichelle wanted to scream at the top of her lungs. "You make me feel so stupid."

"I apologize. That isn't my intention. I don't ever want you to feel stupid, because you're not."

"Then what is it? Are you no longer attracted to me? I'm trying to understand why you don't want me anymore."

"I was under the impression that you didn't want me to want you."

"At first because, Carmelo had just died and I lost my baby, there was so much going on."

"But now?"

"Now, I want to see what can happen between us. I mean, you have me living at your house, but you treat me like a roommate."

"Not so much. I don't do roommates, but if I did and I treated you like one, you would be paying rent and half the utility bills."

"Point taken. So then, what is it? Why haven't you tried to get close to me in an intimate way?"

"Because I respect your wishes. I told you how I felt at the hospital, and you shut me down. So, I decided we could be friends, and I'm actually enjoying our friendship."

"So that's it? We're only gonna be friends?"

"For now, I think that's best. You need to concentrate on school and graduating. If it's meant to happen between us, it will. No need to rush. Call me when you're ready for me to pick you up. I'll already be in the neighborhood."

Nichelle looked out of the window, and realized they were in front of her school. She didn't want to get out the car. There was so much more she wanted to express to Renny, like she wished she had enough guts to say, "I want you to love me", but she didn't.

"Okay," she said, getting out the car, crushed. When she closed the door, she was thinking Renny would call out for her, saying to come back so they could talk, but he didn't. Instead, he drove off, leaving her to go inside to class.

"Tierra, have you decided what classes you're going to take at the community college when school starts back after the summer?"

"Yeah...none!" Tierra answered her mother, as she went through her closet sorting out what clothes she wanted to keep and what items she had no use for.

"I told you that you couldn't stay up in this house not working or going to school. You have to do something productive. I rather you go to school so you can have some better job options."

"No disrespect, but I'd rather do neither."

"So, what you plan on doing then?"

"For the next week or so, I'ma be getting my stuff together so I can move into my new apartment."

"Excuse me?"

"You heard me correctly. It's a great apartment in a high rise in Jersey City, right on the water."

"How in the hell are you going to afford that?"

"I'm house-sitting for a friend."

"You mean some low-life you fuckin', Tierra!"

"I can't believe you being so vulgar! Ain't nobody fuckin'! I did a favor for them, and now they're returning it. It ain't nothin' more than that."

"You know what, Tierra? I'm done. I'm done lecturing you. I'm done tryna make you do something with your life...I'm just done! But when this shit explodes in your face, don't come back knocking on my door, 'cause you ain't gon' get no answer."

"I love you too, Ma," Tierra mumbled sarcastically, and went back to going through her clothes.

Throughout her whole day at school, Nichelle stayed focused on her schoolwork. She figured Mr. Chambers would be cooperative, but she was surprised that each of her other teachers were also being very supportive, and gave her all the assignments that she missed so she could catch up. They seemed impressed that Nichelle even cared enough to try and improve her grades, and they were willing to do all they could to help the cause.

During lunch, instead of hanging out in the cafeteria

or going outside to talk on her phone, Nichelle stayed in the library, doing her work. That was going to be her new routine for the rest of the school year, or at least until she had got completely caught up and was making the sort of grades she wanted.

She had been concentrating so hard on her class work, that it wasn't until the end of the day that she realized she hadn't ran into Lerrick or her crew even once. She still didn't think too much of it, until she heard some girls talking when she went to the bathroom.

"It wasn't just Lerrick, it was Kyla and Cinthia too."

"All three of them?"

"Yep, it happened last week. They made an announcement about it at school. But didn't nobody care. Couldn't nobody stand Lerrick and her crew."

"Do they know who did it?"

"Ain't no telling who killed them bitches. If I knew, I would go shake their hands," the girl said, as she and her friend finished primping in the mirror and walked out of the bathroom.

Nichelle remained in the stall, stunned by what she just heard. She hadn't even used the toilet yet, unable to fully accept as true that Lerrick and the two other girls who participated in holding her as she was beat in the very bathroom she was in right now, were dead. She was so out of it, she almost didn't hear her phone ringing.

"Hello."

"Why haven't you called me? I know school has to be getting out by now."

"Renny, I'm sorry. I was about to call and tell you

to come on."

"Cool, I'll see you in a few."

Nichelle hurried up and used the bathroom, and while washing her hands, she caught a glimpse of herself in the mirror. If you stared long enough, you could see a slight trace of the bruising that hadn't completely gone away from when Lerrick pounded on her face. "Yeah, that bitch did deserve to die," she mouthed, and walked out.

Out Of Your League

If only we could pick and choose who we fell in love with, life would be so less complicated. But then it could also be a lot less pleasurable. Isn't the most intoxicating part about falling in love, is that you don't know who might end up having control over your heart. Especially when he's a street thug with the word danger attached to him.

When Renny picked Nichelle up from school, she wanted to tell him what she found out about Lerrick, but he seemed preoccupied so she kept silent. Then, when they pulled up to the project building where she lived, she hesitated but went ahead and asked what she wanted before getting out the car. "Can you come up with me to my mom's apartment? She wanted to meet you."

"Another time. I have to handle some business across the street. Give your mother my best. Tell her we'll meet soon."

"Are you gonna wait for me, because I wanted to talk to you about something?"

"No. This is what I want you to do. Spend some time with your mother, pack up your belongings, get your car, and meet me at home. We can talk then. But if you need me, you know how to reach me."

"I'll see you later on tonight then." Nichelle got out of the car and briefly watched as Renny drove off before going inside the building. She decided to stop and see Tierra first, and then go to her mother's place.

Nichelle knocked on Tierra's door, and part of her didn't want her to be home because she knew an interrogation would be in the works. She could hear somebody walk up to the door and not say anything, so she knew they were probably looking through the peephole.

When the door opened, at first Tierra didn't say a word. She just gave Nichelle a hug.

"Girl, I have missed you so much! I'm glad you're home...come on in," Tierra said, letting Nichelle go after hugging her for a good minute.

"I missed you too. I'm sorry—"

"You don't have to apologize to me," Tierra put her hand up, cutting Nichelle off. "I heard about what happened with Lerrick, and I completely understand you wanting to stay on the low. But you ain't gonna have to worry about the triflin' bitch no more."

"How did you hear about what happened to her?"

"I was at the beauty salon last week, and her silly ass sister was in there tryna spread lies about you. But I shut that bitch down. She tried to make it seem that you slashed Lerrick's face because you were jealous of her ugly ass...as if!"

"Yeah, I did slash her face, but she deserved it!

She made me lose my baby…Carmelo's baby!" Nichelle couldn't hold back the tears and broke down crying, not over the pain.

"Omigod, Nichelle! I had no idea you lost the baby! Come here." Tierra held her again, this time even tighter, and Nichelle balled like a newborn baby.

"It's been so hard for me. I've never hated anybody as much as I hate Lerrick. I'm glad she's dead."

"Lerrick is dead? When this happen?" Tierra stood back, looking at Nichelle in shock and wanting all the details.

"I heard some girls talking about it today after school in the bathroom. It happened last week. Lerrick, Kyla and Cinthia all got killed. I don't know anymore information other than that. But all three of them played a role in killing my baby. Kyla and Cinthia held me while Lerrick beat the shit out of me in the bathroom at school. I even told that heffa I was pregnant, and she didn't give a fuck! She was straight evil."

Tierra shook her head in disgust. "I wish I would've got to that bitch first and killed her. I know how much you wanted that baby. I'm so sorry, Nichelle."

"Yeah, but I have to let go. I'll always love Carmelo, but he's my past. I have to move on, especially now that I'm no longer carrying his baby."

"So, where have you been? I was worried about you."

"I know, and I should'a called, but I needed some time alone. I've been staying wit' a friend in Jersey."

"Word, what part of Jersey? 'Cause I'ma be doing some house-sitting in Jersey."

"Edgewater."

"I'm in Jersey City. I don't know how far that is from Edgewater. Are you gonna still be staying there? 'Cause if not, you can come stay wit' me. 'Cause I know you don't want to go back to yo' mama's house. I damn sure can't wait to get the fuck outta here. Let's go to my room. I'm packing now. I don't need nothing holding up my progress."

"Actually, I am going back to stay in Edgewater for a little longer. I came to get my clothes, some other stuff, and my car, then I'm going right back."

Tierra was staring at Nichelle strangely. "Did you meet somebody? Don't be holding back on me neither."

"I wasn't gonna` say nothing, but eventually you would find out anyway so I might as well tell you."

"Girl, would you say it? You got me all anxious wanting to know who this mystery guy is."

"Actually, you know him."

"I do? Who is it?"

"Renny O'Neal."

"You talkin' 'bout Radric's friend that we saw at Carmelo's funeral?"

"Yes, can you believe it?"

"No! How the fuck did that happen?"

"I ran into him on my way home after that fight wit' Lerrick. I was fucked up and I started bleeding. He was the one that took me to the hospital. He saved my life."

"I can't believe you're living wit' Renny!" Tierra said, sitting down on her bed with confusion written all over her face.

"I know. I can't believe it either."

"I hope you not falling for him."

"Why you say it like that?"

"Because, Nichelle, he is way out of your league. I'm your girl. I ain't gon' steer you wrong."

"I remember when you were dating Radric, and when Simone was alive, you wanted her to get wit' Renny. You didn't say she was out of his league."

"You know Simone was my girl and I loved her, but she was a trick bitch. She knew how the game rocked. It was about getting as much as you can out a nigga, 'cause you knew that shit wasn't gon' last anyway. I know you, Nichelle. Shit, I practically raised you. You're gonna fall in love wit' him."

"And what's wrong wit' that?"

"See, the fact that you asked me that question lets me know you ain't ready for a nigga like Renny. A nigga like him don't know what love is."

"You're wrong. I'm not saying that he ain't complicated, but he's a good guy."

Tierra put her head down and covered her face with her hand in frustration. "There is nothing good about a man like Renny. I've been around him. I know how he and Radric used to roll. They were heartless."

"Then why did he help me, why has he been so good to me. He hasn't even tried to fuck me."

"Man, that nigga is doin' a number on you. Don't you see it's all calculated? For some reason, Renny has decided that he wants you. If you were a thirsty bitch with nothing to offer but your pussy, I would tell you to ride that gravy train until the wheels fall off. Hell, I would even help you push the shit and make sure you didn't fall until you got everything you could out that nigga. But then, if you were that type of chick, Renny probably wouldn't give you the time of day. So my advice to you is run, Nichelle. Run as fast as you can and don't look back."

"I know you tryna look out for me, and I appreciate that, but I think your wrong about him. Look what Carmelo did to me. Renny couldn't do anything worse than that."

"Chi-i-i-i-ld, compared to Renny, Carmelo was a choir boy. Unfortunately, if you stick around long enough, you'll see. But by then it'll be too late. Because once Renny gets a hold of your heart, even when you see what a monster he is and you want to leave, you won't."

"Tierra, I have to go. My mom is waiting for me. I'll call you later on," Nichelle said abruptly, not wanting to listen to Tierra's warnings about Renny.

"Okay. We have to hang out soon though."

"Of course, especially now that'll we'll both be in Jersey."

Tierra walked Nichelle to the door and gave her a hug goodbye. "Don't be a stranger."

"I won't. We're best friends, that'll never change," Nichelle smiled, and walked out.

Tierra wasn't so sure of that. Out of all the men for Nichelle to get involved with, she hated that it had to be Renny O'Neal. She always felt protective of Nichelle because she wasn't as tough as her and the rest of the girls around the way. But Nichelle would have to learn for herself, and all Tierra could do was be there for her when Renny fucked up, because there was no doubt in her mind that he would.

When Nichelle got back to Jersey, she was surprised but happy that Renny was already home.

"How did everything go with your mom?" Renny asked, putting down the book he was reading.

"Good. She was disappointed that she wasn't able to meet you, but I told her it would happen soon."

"And it will. It was a crazy day for me. There was no way I could've made it happen. But what did you want to talk to me about earlier?"

"Oh yeah, it was a crazy day for me too. I found out that the girls who were responsible for me losing my baby were killed last week."

"I already knew that."

"When did you find out, and who told you?"

"I found out right after it happened, from Kasaun, one of my workers."

"What? How did Kasaun know?"

"Because after he killed them, he informed me that it had been done, since it was me who gave him the order to do it."

Nichelle almost lost her balance and reached for the couch to hold herself up. She got a little dizzy, thinking she wasn't hearing things correctly.

"What did you say?"

"You heard me. Why don't you sit down? You

seem a little shaky."

"You just told me you had one of your workers murder three girls! Don't you think I should be a little shaky?"

"If you say so. Do you want me to get you some water or anything to drink?"

"How can you be so calm? You act like what happened is no big deal!"

"Because to me, it's not. I've known innocent people that have been killed. Do you really believe I gave a second thought to havin' three worthless lives taken out of this world? Plus, you would'a never been able to focus on going to school every day knowing those girls could try to hurt you at any moment. I did everybody a favor by having them erased!" he said, diverting from his normally calm demeanor and getting hyped.

Nichelle couldn't help but think back to her earlier conversation with Tierra. She warned her that Renny was heartless...a monster. But Nichelle rationalized that Renny having Lerrick and her friends killed was him looking out for her, because he cared about her wellbeing. Because he was so calm and unfazed by what happened didn't mean he was heartless, it meant he did what he thought he had to do to protect her.

"I understand why you did it. You've done so much for me. I want to do something for you."

"You are. By going to school, getting good grades and graduating is showing all the gratitude I need."

"I wanna do more."

"Do more, like what?"

"I wanna give you *me*." Nichelle's eyes widened, wondering if what she said touched Renny in any sort of way.

"I already have you," he stated with confidence.

"We've never had sex."

"In your mind we have, and all I need is your mind, and I've been had that."

Nichelle winced inside knowing Renny was hundred percent right. That's why it didn't matter how much Tierra warned her to stay away from him, it was already too late. Her mind was gone. Nichelle needed to be intimate with Renny much more than he needed to be with her, because her mind wouldn't be satisfied until she connected with him on a physical level.

"You're right. I have had sex with you in my mind. But, I want more. I want to feel you inside of me."

"Are you ready for that? Because once we go there, there's no going back. No more talk about Carmelo, or the baby you lost…all that is done. It's about me and us, nothing else. You ready for that?"

Run Nichelle! Run as fast as you can and don't look back! Tierra's warning screamed in her head over and over again, but instead of listening, she ignored it.

"I'm ready. No more looking back. It's all about us," Nichelle said, making it clear that she was down for whatever Renny wanted.

Renny sat back on the couch and reached out his hand without saying a word. But no words were needed. Nichelle knew what was up, and she was dying for Renny to break her off. She stood up, taking off her clothes before going to him.

Renny held her hand and with the other one he glided his finger, outlining every curve on Nichelle's body. He then pulled her down to straddle his lap, and he cupped her breasts as his tongue played with her hardened nipples. Nichelle moaned in satisfaction, and her head went back as the moistness from each kiss brought such gratification to her body.

Renny then slithered his finger inside her pussy until finding the right spot on her clit that had her begging for more. Nichelle grinded her wide hips, her juices drenching his finger. She called out his name in pleasure, reaching an orgasm without even getting a taste of the dick. Her body shivered, and Renny held her close, trying to get her to relax. He then lifted her body, carrying her into his bedroom. When he laid her down, Nichelle thought about the numerous times she dreamed of lying in the bed next to him with her body wrapped around his. Now, it was finally happening.

Nichelle gazed up at Renny as he made love to her with his eyes. When he came out of his clothes, she was about to catch another orgasm from staring at his damn near perfectly crafted body. It looked as if it was hand carved to meet every woman's ideal specifications, all the way down to his massively hung manhood.

When he finally entered her, Nichelle knew it was a complete wrap. He owned her mind, body and soul, but the way his tool filled up her insides, she didn't care. In fact, she welcomed it.

I Hate You

They say it's a thin line between love and hate, but I believe the line just becomes blurry, depending on whether the person in your life is bringing you joy or pain. But, sometimes the love and hate can be so equally powerful they become one in the same. That's when you know you're sprung, and there is no coming back from that.

"Tierra, this crib is official, and the view is beautiful!" Nichelle said, standing in front of the huge bay window in Tierra's bedroom.

"Yeah, it's hot! I'm so fuckin' happy to be out my mom's crib and back to ballin' like I'm supposed to be."

"How long is this house-sitting job supposed to last?"

"I know the lease is paid up for the first year. Hopefully, by the time it's up, my shit will be so lovely, that how I'ma pay for the next year won't even be a stress for me."

"So, who is this new guy that got you living so good—rent paid up, nice ass furniture, cute drop top

BMW? All this shit seemed to have fallen from the sky. Is it that guy you met at the bowling alley a few months back? Did you hit the jackpot wit' him?"

"Yep, it's him."

"So, if he's checkin' for you like this, why don't he just move you in wit' him? It would be much cheaper."

"He's married. And you know wit' them types, I always tax them higher."

"Tierra, don't you ever wanna settle down and—"

"And what, get married? Hell no! These niggas out here ain't shit! And the reason why I know is 'cause I ain't shit neither, and we be out here not being shit together!"

"Girl, you are a straight fool. Always have been, and I've pretty much accepted you always will be."

"Not foolish, logical. I give you a few more years and you'll be logical like me too."

"Whatever. I want to stay just like I am now, in love."

"That didn't take long. But then, we are talkin' about Renny. I'm hardly surprised."

Nichelle blushed. It had only been a couple of months since the first time they made love, and Nichelle had been floating on clouds ever since. She breathed, slept and ate Renny. He consumed her every thought and move. Everything she did was to please him. Her days consisted of going to school and coming home, waiting for Renny.

The only reason she decided to chill with Tierra was because Renny had to go out of town for a day. Missing him had her in such a slump, she thought being around Tierra would cheer her up. It was helping, but she was counting down the minutes, waiting for him to return. "I never thought I could be this happy."

"Humm, if I'm not mistaken, you were so in love wit' Carmelo," Tierra reminded her.

"I realize now that was puppy love. He never had me open like Renny does."

"Oh, so you are aware that dude got you sprung."

"It's that obvious?"

"Pretty much. I am happy for you, Nichelle. But be careful. Renny is a thoroughbred. His kind is damn near extinct. I would be afraid to fuck wit' a nigga like that...and we *know* how I gets down."

"Hold up, that's him calling now. Hey, baby!"

"I called the house and you weren't there. Where are you?"

"At Tierra's. I was missing you and I didn't wanna be alone."

"That's cool."

"When are you coming home? I hate when you're gone."

Tierra wanted to vomit, listening to how mushy Nichelle was being. She didn't know whether to laugh or cry over how far gone Nichelle was.

"I'll be back late tonight, but I have to leave tomorrow again and go to Philly."

"Baby, you leaving me again?" Nichelle was trying not to whine but she couldn't help herself.

"I tell you what. You can come with me."

Nichelle's face instantly lit up.

"During the day, I'll be handling a lot of business.

Bring Tierra so she can keep you company."

"Okay, I'll ask if she wants to come. Thanks, baby. I'll see you tonight."

"He's off the phone, so you can take that smile off your face," Tierra groaned.

"Shut up! But listen, can you go to Philly tomorrow morning? Renny has to handle some business there all day, so he suggested I ask you to come and keep me company."

"Now I'm your babysitter?"

"It'll be fun."

"I'm kiddin'. I'm down."

"It's so nice that Renny is cool with our friendship. Carmelo didn't even want you coming through the front door. That shit was so stressful. Now my best friend and my man is cool...I like that."

"Yeah, Renny ain't a bad nigga. My only concern is you. But if he's making you happy, then fuck it, that's all that matters."

When Nichelle woke up in the morning, the first thing she did was turn around to see if Renny was beside her, and to her relief, he was. She had tried to stay up, waiting for him to come home, but eventually fell asleep. She wanted to wake him, craving to feel him inside of her, but he looked peaceful, so she opted not to.

"I'm starving," she said out loud as she headed to the kitchen. When she opened the refrigerator, there was nothing but the leftover Chinese food she had last night. "Mickey D's still serving breakfast. I'ma go get me something before we head to Philly," she continued, closing the refrigerator door.

Nichelle threw on some jeans and a light sweater. She then grabbed her wallet and house keys, but was confused when she didn't see her car key. Normally she would lay them both on the kitchen counter next to each other. After searching everywhere she thought they could be, she grabbed the keys to one of Renny's cars and went to the garage. Although she figured it was highly unlikely, she was going to peek inside her car to see if she left the key inside.

"What the fuck! Where is my car? I know I parked it right here." Nichelle frantically searched for her car, feeling as if she was losing her mind.

She got back on the elevator and went upstairs. "Renny, wake up...wake up, baby!" she called out, shaking Renny out of his sleep.

"Babe, what is it?" he mumbled, turning around, wanting to go back to sleep.

"Baby, my key is missing and my car is gone! Somebody must'a come in here and stole it! But when? And what we gon' do?"

"We can talk about it when I get up. I'm tired. I just got in a couple hours ago."

"Renny, are you not hearin' what I'm sayin'? Somebody broke in here!"

"Didn't nobody break into shit."

"Then where the fuck is my car?"

"I sold it," Renny stated casually, putting the pillow

over his face, determined to get his sleep on.

"What! You sold it, why? Why would you do some shit like that? I loved that car, and it was a gift from Carmelo!"

Renny slowly moved the pillow from over his face, and slightly lifted his upper body up to face Nichelle. "What did you say?" His voice was steady and even.

Nichelle lowered her tone as if realizing who she was talking to. "I don't understand why you sold my car. You didn't even ask me."

The speed in which Renny reached out and seized Nichelle's arm made her legs buckle and fall down to her knees. "First of all, I told you to never mention Carmelo's name again."

Nichelle swallowed hard, stunned by the fury she could see on Renny's face.

"Second, I don't have to ask you to do anything. I don't want my woman driving around in a car that another man bought her. I should'a been got rid of that shit, but business has been too hectic for me to get around to it."

"I'm sorry," Nichelle whispered in a shivering voice. Renny's grip on Nichelle was so commanding, she couldn't even move.

"When I get some time, you can order a new car, but until then you can drive one of mine, except for the Maserati."

Nichelle nodded her head, not disputing any of what Renny said. But there was no need for him to mention the Maserati. He had already made it known that was his baby, and nobody could drive it but him. "Over there on the dresser you'll see your checking account information. I deposited the money from the sale of the car into your new account. You need to learn how to pay bills and balance money."

"Okay."

"Nichelle, don't ever raise your voice at me unless you willing to back it up. Understood?"

"Yes. I'm sorry, baby."

Renny freed Nichelle's arm and laid down to go back to sleep like nothing happened.

The quick, less than two-hour drive to Philly seemed like an eternity, with the lack of conversation and the dark cloud looming in the car. Tierra didn't know what the fuck was going on, but from the time Renny and Nichelle picked her up, nobody had more than a few words to say.

Damn, I know this nigga gotta Range or some type of truck. Why in the hell did he have to drive this Maserati? This shit sweet as a motherfucker, but I'm cramped like hell back here. Shit, I can't wait to get to Philly and get out this car, 'cause this shit is not comfortable, Tierra thought to herself, eyeing Renny and Nichelle, who both seemed to be in their own misery.

"Renny, how much longer?" Tierra wanted to know.

"Another fifteen minutes."

"Baby, I was thinking maybe we could go out to dinner tonight, after you finished handling your business, of course." Since Tierra was able to get somewhat of a full sentence out of Renny, Nichelle used the opportunity to open up dialogue between them.

"We're gonna have dinner at my cousin's crib," Renny stated, not giving Nichelle any real rhythm.

Tierra was dying to find out what drama jumped off that had the 'hood's royal couple at odds. She sat back, anxiously waiting for them to reach their destination.

Around twenty minutes later, Renny pulled up on the corner of 18th Street and the Parkway, to the Embassy Suites in Center City. He got out of the car not saying a word, and walked into the lobby of the hotel.

"Yo, what the fuck is going on between you and Renny?" Tierra couldn't hold her tongue any longer.

"I don't wanna talk about it." Nichelle's voice sounded like death had hit her.

"What you mean?" Tierra crossed her arms, like you better come with more than that.

"I mean, I don't want to talk about it. I fucked up, and Renny's pissed at me."

"What did you do?"

Nichelle shrugged her shoulders, not wanting to get into the details of what happened. All she wanted was for Renny to stop being mad at her. The silent treatment he was flipping in her direction had her on edge.

"I'll tell you when we get to the room." She decided to fill Tierra in, thinking she could give her some advice on how to make it right.

"Cool, that works, because here come Renny

now."

Nichelle looked up and Renny was walking towards the car with the same distant aura he had when he left. He opened the car door and handed Tierra a room key, and then one to Nichelle. "Your rooms are right next to each other," he said, without making any eye contact.

"You are staying with me tonight, right?"

Tierra wanted to smack the back of Nichelle's head for having that nigga make her sound so pitiful.

"If I wasn't gonna stay wit' you, I would'a left you back in Jersey. I'll be back in a few hours to pick you guys up." He reached in a side compartment and pulled out a stack of bills. "Here, do some shopping, get something to eat, but stay in the vicinity...you understand?"

"Yes."

"Come on, Nichelle, let's go," Tierra said, getting out of the car, tired of witnessing the whole pathetic scene.

"You go 'head. I wanna talk to Renny for a second. I'll meet you upstairs in the room." Tierra rolled her eyes and shut the car door.

"I gotta go," Renny said, brushing Nichelle off.

"Renny, please don't be mad at me anymore. You're right, I should'a never questioned you. It should'a been my suggestion to get rid of the car from jump. It wasn't right for me to be drivin' another man's car, livin' in your crib. That was stupid on my part. It was me being stunned that the car was gone and not knowing what happened, that made me react like that.

I'll never do that again. But I can't take you being mad at me like this. It's driving me crazy!"

"Come here," Renny said, grabbing the back of Nichelle's neck and pulling her toward his mouth. He put his tongue deep down her throat, before gently kissing the top then her bottom lip. "You my baby, you know that."

"Forever. It can't be any other way."

"It won't. Now, go have some fun with Tierra. I'll see you in a few hours."

Nichelle reached over and kissed Renny one more time before getting out the car. The sick feeling that was consuming the pit of her stomach had now vanished since they had kissed and made up.

Nichelle smiled all the way through the lobby to the elevators, imagining the dick-down Renny would give her when they were alone in their hotel room tonight. Her mind had traveled to such an obscene place, that she didn't even notice when a man walked up to her and had been staring at her intently for a few minutes.

"Don't I know you?"

The gentleman's question snapped Nichelle out her daydreaming and caused her to observe the man invading her space. "No, you don't," she cracked, hitting the "up" button on the elevator again.

"Isn't your name Nichelle?"

This time, Nichelle did a long double take, studying the man's face, body and clothes. "How do you know my name?" she asked, being inquisitive and put off at the same time.

"I thought that was you. I never forget an intriguing face."

"Did Tierra put you up to this bullshit?"

"I don't know who Tierra is, but I remember you from the VIP lounge at the bowling alley in Harlem. I gave you my business card."

"Oh yeah, now I remember you. You were tryna sell me dreams of being a model to get in my panties."

"I don't sell dreams, I make them happen. I'm Akil Walker." He extended his hand, but Nichelle gave him no love. "I'm the owner of Pristine Records, and I've branched out with my own men's clothing line. You may or may not have heard of it," he said, knowing if she hadn't, she had been living under a rock.

"You look awfully young to be doing so much." He had a baby face, with a grown man's suit that seemed to have been tailored specifically for his slender build.

"Yep, and I'm about to do a lot more. Starting with introducing my women's line, and I've been looking for a spokes model. The line is cutting-edge-street, with a touch of sexy glamour. And like I told you a few months ago when I first saw you, I believe you'd be perfect."

"So after all this time you ain't found your model? So what, you left New York to patrol the streets of Philly? Interesting," Nichelle smacked.

"Something like that. We've been going to all the major cities, holding open auditions. I don't want a common face that everybody has seen in videos on BET, or their ass has been plastered in *King* or *XXL* magazine. I want a fresh, young but sexy ass woman to rep for my line."

"And you think that's me?"

"I know it is. All I need to do is see if your appeal carries over when you're in front of the camera."

"This sounds somewhat interesting, but I'm here wit' my man for the weekend."

"That's cool, he can come too. Maybe you're not understanding, but this is about business."

"Business, huh?" Nichelle wasn't quite sold on the vision he was selling.

"Here's my business card, again. This time, you should use it. I really can change your life."

Nichelle took the card and put it in her back pocket. The more she listened, something about the dude's swagger made him appear like the real deal. She wasn't hundred percent convinced, but it was worth looking into.

Chanel poured herself a drink, trying to relax since Arnez would be entertaining tonight. She wasn't big on company, preferring to spend her time alone with him, but he was looking forward to having his cousin over. For Chanel, Renny wasn't even the problem. She dug him. But from what she heard, he was bringing his girlfriend and her friend. That was too many females in one room for her liking. She was more of a testosterone type chick than estrogen.

"You look stunning," Arnez complimented Chanel on her black, strapless leather jumpsuit, which accentuated her ample ass to perfection.

"Thank you." Chanel was surprised by Arnez's compliment, since he rarely did so. "How much longer until the guests arrive? Because the sooner they arrive, the sooner they can leave."

"Now, Chanel, I want you on your best behavior. You know how important my cousin is to me."

"Of course. I don't even have a weapon on me. I left it in the bedroom," she winked. Just then, they both heard the knock at the door.

"Right on time," Arnez said, eyeing his watch. "I'm glad you could make it," he smiled, opening the door and letting Renny, Nichelle and Tierra inside.

"I told you I would. You think I'ma be in Philly and not see my people? This is my baby, Nichelle, and her friend, Tierra."

They smiled at Arnez, while Tierra, without so much as pausing, started sizing up his crib and the chick she eyed by the bar.

"Renny's cousin is cute. I guess fineness runs in the family," Tierra whispered to Nichelle.

"Watch yourself. His woman looks like she could take this whole room out with just her stare," Nichelle commented, getting a chill from the ice cold demeanor of Chanel.

"Chanel, don't be rude, come speak to our guests."

Chanel put her drink down and took her time strutting across the floor as if she was doing them a favor by even being in their presence. "It's good to see you again, Renny."

"Likewise. This is my woman, Nichelle, and her friend Tierra."

"Your woman! Is she even legal?" Chanel sulked.

"You ain't fuckin' her, so why you care?" Tierra popped, to one ballsy bitch to another.

Right before Chanel was about to strike, Arnez shut it down. "You have to excuse Chanel. I rarely let her out her cage, and sometimes she doesn't know how to act."

"Well maybe you need to throw her a bone," Tierra mumbled under her breath, but Chanel caught every word.

"That's all good, but Chanel, I do need you to apologize to my woman, because that's what she is. Her age is none of your business."

"Baby, I'm fine. She doesn't have to apologize."

"I'm sorry, Nichelle. That was inappropriate."

"Wonderful. We've all made nice, so let's move on and have dinner." Arnez led everyone to the dinning room, and on there way, Nichelle caught a glimpse of a picture that held her attention and wouldn't let go.

"What a beautiful woman. Who is she?" Nichelle asked, picking up the sterling silver frame from a glass table by the couch."

Chanel wanted to smack Nichelle and the picture out her hand. It infuriated her that Arnez kept that picture out for all to see.

"Her name is Talisa."

"It's amazing how much she looks like my mother when she was younger."

Tierra walked over and took a look. "Damn sure

do. They look like they could be sisters."

"What's your mother's name?" Arnez questioned.

For a brief second, Nichelle was about to say "Teresa", but caught herself.

"You *do* know your mother's name?" Arnez joked.

"Yes, it's Sheila," she answered, putting the picture down.

"Are you okay, baby?" Renny put his arm around Nichelle's waist.

"When you're with me, I'm always okay," she said, sneaking a kiss before they sat down at the dinner table.

After everybody sat down, three servers came out and placed multiple dishes on the table. You had a choice of straight up American cuisine, to French, Italian, sushi, seafood, to good old soul food. Neither Nichelle nor Tierra had ever seen a layout like that before. It was better than being at their favorite all you can eat, ten-dollar buffet in the 'hood, and they never thought it could get better than that.

After a while, everyone was enjoying their meal, music was playing, and the original dark mood had softened. After a couple of more drinks, even Chanel thawed out her icy behavior a tad.

"Where are you going?" Arnez wanted to know when he saw Renny getting up from his chair.

"Over to the bar. You know I'm not a drinker, but I'm in the mood for a little cognac."

"I can have one of the waiters get it for you."

"Man, I know how to pour my own drink."

"Then I'll join you. We can have a drink together."

The two men headed to the bar, and Arnez poured them both a drink while Renny admired the stunning penthouse view.

"Life is truly good. We've been blessed, Arnez."

"Yes, we have," he said, handing Renny his drink. "Sometimes I wake up and can't believe this is my life. I have more money than I can ever spend, and access to the most beautiful women, except the one I want...speaking of beautiful women, Nichelle is breathtaking. You didn't exaggerate one bit. But I have to agree with Chanel, she's extremely young. Do you think she's ready to enter our world and deal with the type of life you live?"

"I've been working on her for months now. It's taken some time, but she's getting there. The fact that she is so young is a plus. I can still mold and train her to be the woman I want."

"I understand you perfectly. If only I had gotten a hold of Talisa at Nichelle's age, how different things would be right now. We would be married with a house full of kids. It might be too late for me, but it's not for you."

"Yeah, but Nichelle's not ready yet. I need some more time to fully break her in. But it'll happen, there's no doubt in my mind.

"Baby, I had so much fun tonight. I've never been to a dinner party like that before. It was all so glamorous and stuff, like how you see on T.V.,"

Nichelle beamed when they got back to their hotel room.

"Yeah, baby, but this is real life. You haven't even seen a glimpse of how me and my people really ball. I'm talking about mansions, private planes, trips to exotic locations where you and your crew are the only ones on the entire island. There is a lot of heat in the streets right now, so we tryna keep shit low-key. But, wait until shit is sweet again…you'll see."

"You call how you livin' now low-key? Damn, and I thought you had me living like a princess!"

"Baby, I'ma have you living like a queen. I gotta get your mind right first."

"My mind is right. I'm totally in love wit' you. What else do you need from me?"

"Don't worry about it. I'll let you know when you're ready."

"I wanna make you happy, baby." Nichelle kissed Renny's chest as he sat on the bed, taking off his pants. Then she worked her kisses down to his dick, and as she held it, massaged it and worshipped every inch of it. "I love this dick, baby, almost as much as I love you."

Renny smirked. "I knew from the second I peeped you, you had primetime potential."

"Seriously?" Nichelle would wrap her lips around Renny's thick dick and deep throat it, then gaze up seeking his approval.

"Yes, and when I'm done with you, you gon' be every nigga's dream bitch. But you belong to me, so it won't even matter."

"Baby, I want you to cum in my mouth. I want to swallow every drop of you."

And that's what Renny did. He exploded in her mouth, and then fucked the shit out of her and exploded inside her pussy. Nichelle couldn't get enough of him. She wanted Renny's dick to rest inside of her until she fell asleep in his arms.

Nichelle woke up in the middle of the night, and like always, the first thing she did was look around for Renny. But this time, he wasn't there and it sent her in a panic. She leaned over to the nightstand and turned on the lamp. She got up to see if he was in the bathroom, but he wasn't. The clothes he had on earlier were missing, and Nichelle's brain went into overdrive. She picked up her cell phone to call him, but saw that he left his in the room. *Where in the fuck can he be!* Nichelle thought to herself as she threw on some clothes and grabbed her room key, not knowing where to begin her search. All she knew was that she wanted Renny back in the bed, sleeping beside her.

As soon as she opened the door, she could clearly hear the voices of two people, and she recognized them as being her best friend and her man. Tierra's room was on the left-hand side, and she peeked her head around and saw Renny's hand slightly holding the door ajar as if he was about to leave. *What the fuck is Renny doing in Tierra's room at this time of night?* She shook her head in uncertainty. *They can't be fuckin' on the low! Oh God, they wouldn't do that to me!*

Nichelle felt like she was going to have a heart

attack right there in the hallway. Instead of jumping to conclusions, she calmed down, and zeroed in on their conversation.

"Tierra, we can finish this when we get back to Jersey. We've spent enough time on this."

"Renny, don't leave yet. I'm not done talkin' to you."

Nichelle noticed Renny letting the door go, and jumped as quiet as she could to catch the door before it closed. She wanted to scream out in pain as two of her fingers, somewhat got smashed, trying to hold it open. She got her bearings together and took a deep breath. She could hear the TV in the back, and knew how Tierra's room was set up. Renny had either gone into the sitting room in front of the bedroom, or went past the double doors into the bedroom. Either way, she figured if she was quiet enough, she could slide her body around the door without being seen and find out what the fuck was going on.

Nichelle's heart was racing. The very idea of Renny and Tierra fucking around was sending her over the edge. When she got in the room and slowly closed the door, neither was in her view, but she could hear their voices. *They must be in the sitting area*, Nichelle reasoned from the direction the sound was coming from. She cracked open the closet door and slid her body inside and tuned in.

"What else do you want from me, Tierra? I put you up in a fully furnished crib, bought you a car, and hit you off wit' plenty of dough. I don't know what else you want from me."

As Nichelle listened, she felt like her entire world was shattering. Her stomach started bubbling and she thought she was going to vomit up everything she had for dinner.

"My concern is that this shit ain't gon' last. I mean, what's gonna happen when I run out of money and you don't want to pay my rent anymore, or my other bills?"

"So what, you want me to maintain your lifestyle forever? Yo, don't be greedy, Tierra. We have an understanding, and you need to stick to it."

"Yeah, our understanding was that you was gon' have Radric and Carmelo set up to be robbed and I would get a cut, not that they would be killed! And let's not forget about Simone and Marley. That was neva part of the understanding. Simone was one of my closest friends."

"But you ain't got no problem spending all the money I hit you off with for doing your part."

"I did. I kept Nichelle busy that night so you could do whatever you was doing."

"Enough of this shit! I don't need for you to give me a play-by-play of what happened. I orchestrated the shit. We gon' come up wit' a number, and after that, I'm done. 'Cause you don't want to end up like your friend, Simone, do you, Tierra?"

"I don't want no problems wit' you, Renny. All I want is to be properly taken care of for the role I played in all this. When we come up wit' a lump sum number, I'ma be good wit' that and not hit you up for no more money, I promise."

Nichelle stormed out the closet in a rage over all that had been revealed to her.

"What the fuck was that noise?" Tierra wondered out loud before catching a glimpse of a distraught Nichelle. "Nichelle! How did you get in here?"

"What you really want to know is, how much did I hear, and the answer is everything! How could you, both of you? Renny, it's one thing for you to kill Lerrick and her friends' because of what they did to me, but Carmelo and Simone? You're a monster!" Renny didn't say a word. Instead, he sat down.

"And you, Tierra! Simone was our friend! You livin' off blood money! But you don't care how you get it, as long as it's gotten! What happened to you? You really believe you've gone from trife life to lavish? Hell no! You still from the gutter! Only difference, instead of doin' dirt in the 'hood, you doin' it in a high-rise. Is livin' some fuckin' lavish life that important to you that you would let innocent people die? I hate you...I hate both of you!" Nichelle broke down in tears and ran out of the room, slamming the door.

"Aren't you gonna go after her?" Tierra asked Renny, who was sitting down composed as if nothing happened, where as Tierra's hands were shaking. She was devastated that Nichelle now knew the truth.

"She needs time alone. I'll give her that."

"Excuse me! Time alone? Yo, she found out that you had four people wiped out, including a man she was in love wit'!"

"Nichelle is in love wit' me. Carmelo is of no relevance. She'll be back, she has no choice. I'm all she knows."

"I warned Nichelle about you. Now she's seen it for herself...you're heartless."

"You better hope that isn't true, because if it is, that doesn't leave you in a very promising position, now does it."

The next morning when Renny woke up, Nichelle still hadn't returned. He wasn't shocked, but extremely disappointed. He felt his grip on her was strong enough that eventually she would come back to him, but he wasn't a patient man. And the longer Nichelle made him wait, the more severe her punishment would have to be once she returned.

"So, we just gon' leave Philly without Nichelle?" Tierra complained as they walked down to the hotel parking garage.

"There's no need in us staying. Nichelle ain't coming back here."

"How is she gonna get home? She don't know nothing about Philly."

"She'll find her way home. If not, she'll call."

"So, you gon' just let her be. You know how sweet Nichelle is. She ain't gon' be able to make it out here...or maybe she will," Tierra said, changing her tune when she saw the gift Nichelle left for Renny.

His prized Maserati was destroyed. The tires were slashed and all the windows and headlights were busted. She even keyed the entire car, and just so there wasn't any doubt who was responsible for the mayhem, she left a note taped to the busted front winshield, saying, *"I Hate You! Love, Nichelle."*

Genesis

If you had a chance to right all the wrongs you've done, would you take it? Would you grab hold of the opportunity to forsake yourself and save another? Or would you continue on your dismal path of self-destruction?

When Nichelle stood up from the makeup chair and walked out of her dressing room into the studio, she felt confident. The white, boy shorts with matching jacket that had fur trim around the collar and sleeves, fit like it was created to grace her body. The stiletto heels on the long white boots that hugged her legs clicked on the hardwood floor as she prepared for her debut.

"I'm ready," she told the man behind the camera, knowing that all eyes were on her.

"Bring the panther in," he directed one of his assistants.

A few minutes later, the trainer came out with the most beautiful Black Panther—scratch that—animal that Nichelle had ever seen. He had piercing yellowish-green eyes, which made the whole room come alive. The trainer positioned the panther right where the photographer wanted, and Nichelle stood near the panther as if she had raised him since he was a newborn.

"Let's do this," Nichelle said, dropping down right behind the panther, placing one hand across her thigh and the other playfully cupping her curvaceous ass. As the lights flashed each time the photographer took her picture, she gave her million-dollar pose like her life depended on it.

"I knew she was the one," Akil said, standing behind the photographer, while relishing in his triumph of hand picking a girl out of oblivion and turning her into the spokes model of his women's clothing line.

While Nichelle maintained perfect professionalism in front of the camera, her mind wandered back to what had brought her there...two of the most important people in her life deceiving her. Although it had been weeks since she first found out about the horrific role each played in the deaths of four people—two who Nichelle cared a great deal about—it seemed like yesterday. A moment never seemed to go by that she wouldn't find herself replaying some part of the conversation she heard between Renny and Tierra, and each time, she would get angrier and angrier.

Wandering the streets of Philly and not knowing a soul, but determined not to return to Renny, Nichelle found the business card in her pocket and decided to call. Originally, it wasn't even about the modeling gig. She wanted his help to get back to New York. But soon Akil convinced her that if she listened to him and followed his lead, her billboard would be plastered in

Times Square. With nothing to lose and everything to gain, Nichelle said, fuck it, and now here she was.

But, Nichelle couldn't lie to herself and pretend that there wasn't a part of her dying inside from missing Renny. What made it worse, was that he hadn't reached out to her once.

Tierra had been blowing up her phone and left a ton of messages, but nothing from Renny. Even though it had been Renny who did the unforgivable, he was able to make Nichelle feel that somehow it was her fault they weren't together. She hated that he had that sort of hold on her, mentally. Nichelle was well aware that eventually she would no longer be able to escape having it out with Renny. But she prayed the longer it took, the stronger she would become.

"That's a wrap!" the photographer yelled out, bringing Nichelle out of the depressing journey she was taking with Renny on her mind.

"You did phenomenal!" Akil said, giving Nichelle a hug. "You were better than I imagined. I'm proud of you. You showed up and showed out. We got a star right here, people!" Akil pointed his finger at Nichelle, boasting to everybody in the room.

"Thanks for believing in me, Akil, because if you hadn't, I wouldn't be standing here right now."

"I know, but you ain't seen nothing yet. This is only the beginning. We're going places, you'll see."

"Who would'a ever thought that I would be a star. Wow, Genevieve, look how far you've come."

"Genevieve? Who is that?" Akil stared at Nichelle in bewilderment.

"Oh, don't mind me. I was thinking of a little girl I knew from a long time ago. But, umm, although I do believe we're going places, right now, the only place I want to go to is back to my hotel room."

"I understand. You worked your ass off today. Go get some rest and I'll see you tomorrow. The driver will be out front waiting for you when you're ready."

"Thanks."

Nichelle closed her eyes and sat back as the chauffer-driven Town Car headed to her hotel in midtown Manhattan. She was so tired that she barely heard her cell phone ringing. She didn't recognize the 718 number and ignored it. But whoever it was, kept calling back. "Hello!"

"Yes, is this Nichelle Martin?"

"Who wants to know?" Nichelle couldn't identify the female voice on the other end and was tempted to hang up.

"This is Rita, calling from Elmhurst Hospital."

"Oh my God! What happened? Is it Renny?" Nichelle cried, becoming panic-stricken.

"I don't know a Renny. It's your mother. You need to get here right away."

Nichelle dropped her phone. "Go to Elmhurst Hospital, *now!*"

By the time Nichelle got to the hospital, she was beyond distraught. Luckily, once she got inside, a few nurses could see how visibly shaken she was, and were kind enough to take her to the right location.

When she got to her mother's room, her head was wrapped in bandages and she had tubes coming from every direction. She literally seemed to be on her deathbed.

Nichelle bent down next to her mother's bed and the tears flowed. She was tired of crying. It seemed her life was full of one never-ending tragedy after another.

"Oh, Ma! What happened? Who did this to you?"

"My baby, I been holding on, hoping you would make it in time."

Nichelle could see a single tear falling down her mother's face. It was evident how much pain she was in. "I'm here now. Who did this?"

"I don't have much time, but I have to tell you this before it's too late and please forgive me, baby."

"Tell me what?"

"You have a brother, and his name is Genesis... Genesis Taylor. Last time I saw him, he was in a juvenile detention in Pemberton, New Jersey. You were just a baby then."

"I have a brother?"

"Yes, and I want you to find him. He's the only person that's gonna be able to protect you. Your life is in danger. The people who shot me are coming after you next."

"Who shot you, Ma? Tell me!"

Her mother began shaking, and her breathing was becoming erratic. "Nurse! Nurse, get in here! My mother needs a doctor!" Nichelle screamed out. She was holding on to her mother's hand, but she could feel the life in her slipping away.

"Miss, we need you to leave!" one of the nurses ordered.

"Please, save my mother!" Nichelle screamed out again.

"We're going to do all that we can, but you have to exit the room now."

Nichelle leaned against the wall, falling to her knees. "Dear God, no-o-o-o! Not my mother!" She wrapped her arms around her shoulders, trying to numb the pain, but it didn't work. When the doctor and the nurses came out, they didn't have to tell her anything. Her mother was gone. It seemed that death was following her.

When Nichelle left the hospital, she took a taxi to her mother's place. She needed answers, and believed the only place she would find them was there. She unlocked the door, and everything seemed to be intact. Whoever harmed her mother didn't do so in her home.

She ran to the back to where her mother's room was and started going through the drawers and the closet, wanting to find a picture, a letter…anything that would lead her to her brother. *I can't believe it! I have a brother! An older brother, and his name is Genesis, and I'm Genevieve. I will find him. I've lost so much, it's time I gain something,* Nichelle thought as she continued going through her mother's things, searching for a clue.

As she continued rummaging through things, she heard a knock at the door that soon turned into pounding. She went into the kitchen and grabbed a knife, remembering the warning her mother gave her. When she looked in the peephole, she saw the familiar face, and at first wasn't going to answer the door.

"Nichelle, if you're in there open up!" Tierra yelled. "Please, Nichelle. Renny sent me." Nichelle reluctantly opened the door. "Thank goodness you're here!" Tierra sighed when she saw Nichelle.

"What do you want, Tierra?"

"I'll tell you when we get in the car. It's too much, and I don't have time to stand here and explain. Get your stuff and come on."

"But I'm looking for something."

"Yeah, whatever it is, I'm sure it has to do with your brother, Genesis."

"How did you know?"

"There's a lot I know, but come on, we have to go!"

Nichelle grabbed her purse and followed Tierra. "Where's Renny? Why didn't he come?"

"He wanted to, but some serious shit is goin' down, so he sent me. He gave me clear instructions for me to bring you directly to him. And I'm not fuckin' this up, 'cause you already know my ass is grass if I do."

"Since you know about Genesis, I take it you know about my mother too."

"Yeah, I'm so sorry, Nichelle. I know how much you loved your mother and how much she loved you."

"Everything is bananas. I feel like I'm walking in somebody else's world right now, like this ain't even my life. And yo, how far away did you park?"

"We're almost there," Tierra said, picking up her pace as they made their way to her car.

"Are they with you?" Nichelle was the first to notice they had company.

"Who?" Tierra questioned before seeing who it was.

"Nichelle, Tierra, I'm glad I caught you."

"Arnez, what are you doing here?" Tierra asked with uneasiness in her voice.

"Renny sent me. He wanted you ladies to come with me." Then Chanel stepped from behind the truck, looking icy as ever.

"Oh, and he wanted you to bring Chanel too?" she asked sarcastically. Tierra grabbed Nichelle's wrist, keeping her by her side. "We're fine. Renny asked me to bring Nichelle to him, and that's what I'm gonna do. But I'll let him know you offered to help."

"Tierra, I'm only going to tell you this once. I want you and Nichelle to get in the car, *now!*" Arnez demanded.

"Nichelle, run…*now!*" Tierra kicked Arnez in his groin area as hard as she could, trying to give Nichelle an opportunity to get away.

Chanel swung into motion to catch up with Nichelle, but Tierra was too quick and put her foot out, tripping Chanel, who fell to the concrete.

"Tierra, come on! I don't want to leave you!" Nichelle screamed out, looking back as she sprinted down the dark street

"I'm right behind you!" Tierra shouted.

When Nichelle turned back around, to her relief, Tierra was hauling ass, coming in her direction. Nichelle kept pounding the pavement, moving full speed ahead while searching for safety, until she heard a gunshot. She slowed her pace down, turned around, and from the distance she could see Tierra's body hitting the ground.

"No-o-o-o-o-o-o-o-o!" Nichelle's voice echoed throughout the entire Queens project.

It took everything inside of Nichelle not to go back for her best friend, but the very sacrifice Tierra made was so that Nichelle could go free. So Nichelle ran, and she wouldn't stop running until she ran right into her brother's arms.

Want the full story behind Nichelle's (Genevieve) brother (Genesis...read Stackin' Paper

P.O. Box 912
Collierville, TN 38027

A KING PRODUCTION

www.joydejaking.com
www.twitter.com/joydejaking

ORDER FORM

Name:

Address:

City/State:

Zip:

QUANTITY	TITLES	PRICE	TOTAL
	Bitch	$15.00	
	Bitch Reloaded	$15.00	
	The Bitch Is Back	$15.00	
	Queen Bitch	$15.00	
	Last Bitch Standing	$15.00	
	Superstar	$15.00	
	Ride Wit' Me	$12.00	
	Ride Wit' Me Part 2	$15.00	
	Stackin' Paper	$15.00	
	Trife Life To Lavish	$15.00	
	Trife Life To Lavish II	$15.00	
	Stackin' Paper II	$15.00	
	Rich or Famous	$15.00	
	Rich or Famous Part 2	$15.00	
	Rich or Famous Part 3	$15.00	
	Bitch A New Beginning	$15.00	
	Mafia Princess Part 1	$15.00	
	Mafia Princess Part 2	$15.00	
	Mafia Princess Part 3	$15.00	
	Mafia Princess Part 4	$15.00	
	Mafia Princess Part 5	$15.00	
	Boss Bitch	$15.00	
	Baller Bitches Vol. 1	$15.00	
	Baller Bitches Vol. 2	$15.00	
	Baller Bitches Vol. 3	$15.00	
	Bad Bitch	$15.00	
	Still The Baddest Bitch	$15.00	
	Power	$15.00	
	Power Part 2	$15.00	
	Drake	$15.00	
	Drake Part 2	$15.00	
	Female Hustler	$15.00	
	Female Hustler Part 2	$15.00	
	Female Hustler Part 3	$15.00	
	Female Hustler Part 4	$15.00	
	Female Hustler Part 5	$15.00	
	Female Hustler Part 6	$15.00	
	Princess Fever "Birthday Bash"	$9.99	
	Nico Carter The Men Of The Bitch Series	$15.00	
	Bitch The Beginning Of The End	$15.00	
	Supreme...Men Of The Bitch Series	$15.00	
	Bitch The Final Chapter	$15.00	
	Stackin' Paper III	$15.00	
	Men Of The Bitch Series And The Women Who Love Them	$15.00	
	Coke Like The 80s	$15.00	
	Baller Bitches The Reunion Vol. 4	$15.00	
	Stackin' Paper IV	$15.00	
	The Legacy	$15.00	
	Lovin' Thy Enemy	$15.00	
	Stackin' Paper V	$15.00	
	The Legacy Part 2	$15.00	
	Assassins	$11.00	

Shipping/Handling (Via Priority Mail) $7.50 1-2 Books, $15.00 3-4 Books add $1.95 for ea. Additional book.
Total: $_____ FORMS OF ACCEPTED PAYMENTS: Certified or government issued checks and money Orders, all mail in orders take 5-7 Business days to be delivered

CPSIA information can be obtained
at www.ICGtesting.com
Printed in the USA
LVHW020107090721
692195LV00004B/454